This Island
Isn't Big Enough
for the Four of Us!

Gery Greer and Bob Ruddick

This Island Isn't Big Enough for the Four of Us!

HarperTrophy
A Division of HarperCollinsPublishers

F
Gre

Library of Congress Cataloging-in-Publication Data
Greer, Gery.
  This island isn't big enough for the four of us.

  Summary: Pete and Scott excitedly plan a
camping trip to a deserted island, only to arrive
and discover that two girls with zany senses of
humor are already in residence.
  [1. Camping—Fiction]   I. Ruddick, Bob.
II. Title.
PZ7.G85347Th 1987   [Fic]   86-47750
ISBN 0-690-04612-X
ISBN 0-690-04614-6 (lib. bdg.)

  (A Harper Trophy book)
ISBN 0-06-440203-7 (pbk.)

Published in hardcover by HarperCollins Publishers.
First Harper Trophy edition, 1989.

16001

To Stephen

This Island
Isn't Big Enough
for the Four of Us!

1

My best friend, Pete McKenzie, was a little upset. I could tell because his eyes were bulging and because he had me by the shirt collar and was shaking me.

"It's for *babies*!" he sputtered. "It's a *baby's* tent! I wouldn't be caught dead in it!"

I could understand his point of view. It *was* a baby's tent, and I didn't exactly want to be caught dead in it myself. But I wasn't about to admit it.

"Pete," I said, "be reasonable. You're jumping to conclusions. I tell you what. Let's have another look at it."

He let go of my collar, and we both stood back and had another look.

"It's a sissy tent!" he yelled.

"No," I countered, "it's just colorful, that's all. It's got character. I think I kind of like it."

It was bad, all right. Very bad. Any other tent in the world would have been a big improvement. But the sad fact was that we were stuck with it. I had promised to borrow a tent, and unfortunately this was the tent I'd borrowed. As soon as I'd gotten it, I'd set it up in my backyard and then called Pete on the phone and asked him to come over and see it. Naturally, he came right away. Naturally—because starting the next day, this tent was going to be our home for seven days.

Starting the next day, Pete and I were going to begin the adventure of our dreams—camping out alone on a wild, uninhabited island in the middle of a remote lake. For a whole week. Just Pete and me and the wilderness.

And, of course, our tent. Our very own Hänsel and Gretel's Gingerbread House Tent. The deluxe model. The first in a new line of "Tiny Tot Tents for Backyard Camping." The cutest, sweetest, most lovable tent ever made.

"It's goofy!" yelled Pete. "Look at it. It's got little windows with frilly curtains. It's got a chimney with candy canes on it. It's got *frosting* on its roof!"

"Yeah," I said. "But look, it's big enough for us to stand up in."

Pete glared at me. "The doorknob," he said grimly, "is a big cookie with a face painted on it."

I guess you could say it was my fault about the tent. But actually, all I did was agree to do my Uncle Ted a favor. Uncle Ted works for this company that designs camping equipment, called Gray Wolf Backcountry Supplies. And naturally, when he asked me if Pete and I would field-test a tent for him, I said yes. I just assumed it'd be one of your regulation heavy-duty, rough-and-ready, explorer-type tents.

How could I have known that someone had come up with this Tiny Tot Tents idea?

Besides, Uncle Ted was also lending us two brand-new sleeping bags, a bunch of waterproof duffel bags, and a sixteen-foot aluminum canoe. It seemed only fair that we should do him a favor in return.

"What's this?" demanded Pete suddenly.

He was bending over a piece of rolled-up plastic attached to the tent at the base of the door. Before I could stop him, he started backing away from the tent, unrolling it onto the ground.

"That's our sidewalk," I explained.

It had little round cobblestones painted on it. And a grass trim on either side. Little plastic tulips sprang up as he unrolled it.

Pete straightened up and folded his arms across his chest. "I'm not going," he said.

I wasn't exactly surprised by Pete's reaction. Ever since we'd gotten permission to go on this trip, he'd been picturing himself as some sort of rugged backwoodsman or old-time explorer or something. According to Pete, this wasn't going to be just an ordinary camping trip. This was High Adventure. This was our big chance to leave behind the namby-pamby comforts of home and survive on our own. To tame nature with our bare hands. To pit our wits against the elements—and win.

There'd be a bonus, too. When we started school at Franklin Junior High in September, we'd have tanned faces and rippling muscles. And there'd be a strange light in our eyes. One look at us and the other kids would whisper to each other, "Those two have laughed in the face of danger!"

At least, that was Pete's theory.

As for me, I figured I'd be happy if we just did a little swimming, a little fishing, and a little exploring. And if we got some clear nights, I was hoping I could use my binoculars to make a few simple astronomical observations. Like checking out the great galaxy in Andromeda, the great globular cluster in Hercules, and the Cygnus star cloud. Astronomy's a big interest of mine, so I was planning to take along my *Astronomy with Binoculars* book and my best star map, too.

Of course, none of this was going to happen unless I could convince Pete not to let a little thing like a Tiny Tot Tent with frosting on its roof stand in the way of High Adventure.

"Look, Pete," I reasoned, "what difference does it make what the tent looks like? There won't be anyone else on the island to see it."

Pete still looked grumpy, but he couldn't argue with that. We'd done some research on Turtle Island, and as far as we could learn, no one ever went there. There were a few cabins along the shore of the lake, but the island itself was totally wild.

"Maybe," he grumbled, eyeing the candy canes, "but it's the principle of the thing. How could anyone sleep in there without feeling like a two-year-old?"

"We don't actually have to sleep in it," I pointed out. "We can just set it up and store our stuff inside, and only sleep in it if it rains."

"I don't know . . ." said Pete, weakening.

"Besides," I went on, "we don't have time to

5

borrow another tent before tomorrow. And we can't postpone the trip. What if our parents got cold feet and called the whole thing off?"

Pete thought it over, muttering to himself and kicking at a tulip.

It hadn't been easy talking our parents into letting us go in the first place. Two twelve-year-old boys camping out alone? Too dangerous, they'd said. We'd freeze or starve or drown or get eaten alive before the first day was over. But Pete and I didn't give up. We started working on them at the beginning of the summer and kept at it, slowly wearing them down. And just to let them know we were really serious, we took a three-week course in canoeing down at the YMCA.

The big break finally came when my parents volunteered to spend their vacation at a small, rickety old lodge right on the shore of Lost Lake. That way Pete and I could stay on Turtle Island, about three quarters of a mile out in the lake. If we ran into any trouble, we promised we'd send up emergency signal flares.

So everybody was happy. Pete's mother, who'd grown up on a cattle ranch in Montana, said she guessed maybe this was a good opportunity for us to learn a little self-reliance in the great out-doors—and Pete's father agreed with her. Meanwhile, my father said he looked forward to getting in a little serious fishing, and my mother said she could use the peace and quiet to catch up on the book reviews she writes.

Pete and I might never get another chance like this—and Pete knew it.

"What's it like inside?" said Pete, frowning at the gumdrops around the door of the tent. He pulled open the flap and peered in.

"I wouldn't go in there—" I tried to warn him.

Pete disappeared inside. I didn't think he was going to be very happy to find out that the inside was painted, too. It looked just like the inside of a cozy little cottage.

A muffled croak came from inside the tent. "A *witch*?"

I guess he'd seen the wicked witch painted on the wall over by the painted fireplace. She had a big, sugary smile on her face and was holding a platter of cupcakes.

On the front of her black dress, right over her heart, she was wearing a small, white badge. It had colorful little lettering that said,

> Don't be naughty, don't be mean.
> Keep your hands and facey clean.

"*Facey?*" yelled Pete in an outraged voice. He came charging out of the tent. "*Facey?*" he demanded.

7

I should have known better than to joke at a time like this, but I couldn't help it.

"That's right, Pete," I said very seriously. "And don't forget to wash behind your earsies, too."

Pete wouldn't speak to me for the next half hour.

2

Without warning, Pete suddenly stopped paddling and laid his paddle across the bow of our canoe. Throwing his arms open wide, he looked out across the lake toward our destination: Turtle Island.

"O noble island!" he called out. "O island of great mystery and danger!"

Oh, brother, I thought, rolling my eyes. Here we go again. Pete has what my mother calls "a flair for the dramatic," and all morning long he'd been in top form. He even looked the part. The week before, he'd rummaged around all the secondhand stores down on First Street till he'd found an old buckskin shirt with fringe across the shoulders and a bone hunting horn with a leather strap. And naturally, since this was the first day of our big adventure, he was wearing them both.

"O island of the deep dark forest!" he went on. "O island of—"

"O Pete," I broke in. "O Pete, old buddy. Do you think you could do a little less talking and a little more paddling?"

"Land of the grizzly bear! Land of the buffalo! We are coming!"

Land of the *buffalo*? There probably wasn't a buffalo within a thousand miles, or a grizzly bear either. But that was Pete for you. Always hoping for the best. Always hoping for a little death-defying adventure—just to liven things up.

He gave a long blast on his hunting horn. "Forward ho!" he said, and began paddling again.

"Right," I said, joining in. The canoe leaped forward.

Actually, I have to admit I was as excited as Pete. After all those weeks of planning, we were finally on our way. It had felt great to push off from the half-sunken old pier in front of the lodge. Pete had given my parents a solemn farewell. "Do not suffer with heavy hearts," he said gravely. "When the sun has risen a thousand times more, we shall return."

"Make that a week," my father had said. "And remember, you guys had better come back alive or you're going to be in very big trouble."

Now, a quarter of an hour later, here we were, on our own, slicing through the clear blue water of Lost Lake.

Pete stopped paddling again.

"Where do you think we ought to land?" he asked me.

I shielded my eyes from the sun and peered out at the island. Pete hadn't been far wrong when he'd called it the "island of the deep dark forest." Practically all I could see was trees. For almost the whole length of the island—about a mile and a half from north to south—a thick forest crowded right up to the rocky shore. There were no signs of civilization. No people, no campsites, no nothing. Pete and I had never seen Turtle Island before except on maps, but we'd picked it because we'd wanted a wild, untouched island—and it looked like we were going to get it.

"How about that cove near the south end?" I said, pointing to a small cove with a short stretch of sandy beach. Behind it was a sunny clearing.

"Looks good," said Pete. "But maybe we should give it a name first."

"Okay," I said. "Got any ideas?"

One of the things Pete and I planned to do during our week was to map the island and name all the features. And when it came to thinking up names, I knew I could count on Pete. He has one of those active imaginations you always hear about.

"How about Cove of the Screaming Ghost?" he suggested.

See what I mean?

"Perfect," I said.

Pete gave another blast on his hunting horn, and together we started paddling again.

There wasn't any excuse for what happened. I mean, all we had to do was land the silly canoe on the silly island.

And we were almost there, too. Gliding into the cove without a hitch, riding high. Everything seemed great. The sun was shining, the water was sparkling, and the smell of wildflowers filled the air. Off to our left a fish jumped.

This is the life, I told myself.

Then, suddenly, Pete stood straight up in the front of the canoe, raised his paddle, and pointed it at the island. The canoe wobbled around like crazy.

"Many moons it has been . . ." he began in a booming voice.

12

"Down in front!" I sputtered, struggling wildly to steady the canoe.

". . . since we have come to these lonely shores! Behold! It is I, the mighty Pete McKenzie. Friend of the Eagle, Brother of the Moose!"

He flourished his paddle in my direction, and the canoe almost went over. My paddle flipped out of my hand, whacked me on the chin, and fell overboard.

"And," he went on grandly, "my loyal companion, Scott Wilson. Friend of the Bear, Brother of the Duck! Hear us, O island! We greet thee!"

I thought about lunging to the front of the canoe and tackling him below the knees, but I never got the chance. Because just then I heard some strange snortling sounds coming from somewhere on the shore.

I wheeled around on my seat, and what I saw made my blood run cold. My mouth dropped open and my stomach turned into a two-ton ball of cement.

There, half hidden behind a clump of bushes, watching our every move, were two girls! Two girls about our age. Two girls who were *laughing their heads off*.

For one awful moment, time seemed to freeze, and I took in the whole horrible scene.

The tall athletic one, with long blond hair and

a T-shirt with a picture of a hang glider on it, was pointing at us with one hand and clutching her friend's shoulder with the other. That was to keep from falling down, she was laughing so hard.

The shorter one had her dark-brown hair in a ponytail, and was wearing cutoffs and a blue plaid shirt. I couldn't tell what she looked like because half her face was covered by the camera she was holding up to her eye. But under the camera, there was a huge grin on her face that seemed to say, "This has got to be the funniest pair of nincompoops I've ever seen in my life."

The camera was pointed at us.

"Lo!" Pete was bellowing at the top of his lungs. "We have come from across the stormy seas!"

I tried to keep calm. The girl obviously hadn't taken the picture yet, so I forced a sickly little smile onto my face.

"Pete!" I hissed out of the corner of my mouth. "Pe-ete!"

He didn't hear me.

"Watch this!" he said. And he leaped out of the canoe.

He was aiming for a large, flat rock that jutted out from the shore into the deep water of the cove. I guess he figured this was his chance to make a dramatic landing. But he hadn't counted on the way the canoe shot out from under him when he pushed off, so he was a little short of the mark. His toes caught the edge of the rock, all right, but he didn't have enough momentum to carry him any farther.

For a few seconds he just sort of hung there, flapping his arms in big circles like a windmill, trying to make headway. Then he fell backward in a perfect arc, still flapping, the fringe on his buckskin shirt flying.

I wasn't ready for the splash he made. It caught the canoe broadside, and in one quick motion the canoe flipped over. Whoops of loud laughter came from shore as I somersaulted through the air and hit the water, leading with the top of my head. The last thing I saw before I went under was my own feet, high up in the air. Two green tennis shoes against the blue sky.

Oh, dandy, I thought to myself with disgust as I swam back up to the surface. This is just dandy.

Pete and I couldn't have done better if we'd gone to clown school.

3

It took the girls a good five minutes to stop laughing. Finally, the one with the ponytail gave one last chortle, wiped the tears from her eyes, and sighed.

"Now let me see," she said, smiling sweetly at Pete and me. "Which one of you is the Brother of the Moose, and which one is the Brother of the Duck?"

That set them off again. They cracked up and practically fell off the boulder they were sitting on. They'd moved close to the beach while we'd been splashing around, rescuing our gear from the water. I guess they wanted a front-row seat.

Pete and I tried to ignore them. We exchanged a long, disgusted look, just to show we were above such childish behavior. Then we gathered our stuff together and checked it over. Luckily, we'd packed all our supplies in waterproof bags, so everything was dry. Except us, of course. We were soaking wet. Every time we moved, our tennis shoes made loud squishing noises.

"Care to see your pictures, guys?"

It was the dark-haired one with the ponytail again. She seemed to be the leader, and had a challenging way of looking at you, like she knew what you were thinking or something. She had a color photograph in each hand.

"Oh, no," I groaned quietly.

Pete froze, right in the middle of trying to wring out the corner of his buckskin shirt. "Pictures? Of us?"

"Sure," she said, chin up and blue eyes twinkling. "I got one of each of you. With my Polaroid. Want to see?"

Her friend with the hang glider T-shirt giggled. "Yeah, take a look," she urged. "They're great. Jill got each of you just as you hit the water!"

Now that I think about it, I guess that's when I should have gotten tough. After all, there are times to be nice and there are times to be tough.

This was a time to be tough. I probably should have looked this Jill girl right in the eye and said something like, "Okay, sweetheart. Get this and get it good. You're gonna fork over those pictures right now, or I'm gonna smash that fancy little camera of yours into a million fancy little pieces!"

But instead, all I said was, "Thanks, but we don't much care for snapshots, do we, Pete?"

I could feel my ears turning red. Why'd I have to say *that*?

Pete, meanwhile, had been moving slowly closer to the girls, sort of leaning forward like a bird dog on the scent, trying to get a better look at the pictures. When he got about three feet away he stopped, gaped at them for a second, and then choked. He made a grab for them.

Jill whisked them behind her back.

"Now, now," she scolded. "Mustn't take things that don't belong to you. Besides, we're very fond of these pictures. We're going to frame them— and keep them always."

Making sure to keep them out of Pete's reach, she passed one of them to her friend. "Here, Sunny," she said. "You can have Mr. Moose. I'll take Mr. Duck."

They burst into giggles again.

That did it. A guy can only take so much. I charged over and stood next to Pete.

18

"Look, you two," I blurted. "Don't you have anything better to do? Pete and I are kind of busy."

"Yeah," put in Pete. "Why don't you just get in your rowboat or whatever you came in and go back where you came from?"

"Yeah, this is *our* island," I added, sort of stretching things a little.

"*Your* island?" said Jill, raising her eyebrows. "What makes it your island? We were here first. Maybe *you* should leave."

"Leave, my foot," snapped Pete. "We're going to be camping here for the next week."

"Oh, good," said Sunny as she hooked her long blond hair behind her ears. "We're going to be here about nine days ourselves. Maybe we can go fishing together or something."

Pete and I stared at her.

"*You're camping on the island?*" croaked Pete. "I thought you were just here for a picnic or something."

"No, we've been here since yesterday," said Sunny matter-of-factly. "We're camping on the other side of the island, with Jill's Aunt Katherine. We've got a great spot, too, right next to the water."

Pete and I stared at each other. Camping on *our island*? Two girls camping on *our island*? We

19

were stunned. How were we going to tame the wilderness with our bare hands and laugh in the face of danger with *them* around?

"Well," said Jill cheerfully, sliding off the boulder and readjusting the camera strap on her shoulder, "unless you guys are going to do some more water sports, I guess we'd better be going."

"Yeah," said Sunny. "Jill's aunt said maybe she'd show us how to build a bird blind before she goes on her owl watch tonight. She's a wildlife photographer, you know." They started off across the clearing, with Jill in the lead. "See you later," chirped Sunny.

Pete and I stood there, speechless, watching them go. They sauntered off looking carefree and unconcerned, as if it were all in a day's work to horn in on someone else's island and crush their dreams of glory. Not to mention watching us make complete fools of ourselves.

Why can't they trip over their own feet or something? I thought to myself as they neared the woods. Why can't they run into a tree? Why can't they—

Jill stopped and turned around.

She studied the photograph in her hand for a few seconds and then looked up again.

"Oh, Mr. Du-uck," she called in a singsong voice.

I think she was referring to me.

20

"Mr. Duck," she continued sweetly, "may I give you a little advice? You really could improve your diving a hundred percent if you'd just keep your legs straight and remember to point your toes."

Before I could open my mouth to answer, she turned, and the two of them disappeared into the woods, giggling up a storm. I could feel my ears getting red again.

I glanced over at Pete. He looked grim. His lips were pressed together, and his eyes were narrowed. Even though his buckskin shirt was still dripping wet, he looked like a frontiersman. A frontiersman with a purpose.

"You know what this means, don't you?" he said grimly. "This means war."

"Right," I said just as grimly. "Our honor's at stake."

Nothing more needed to be said. It was decided.

Somewhere on Turtle Island there were two girls who were going to wish they'd never tangled with a certain Mr. Moose and Mr. Duck.

4

Silently I slithered up to the crest of the hill, pulling myself along the ground with my elbows, commando-style. Pete was a little behind me because the fringe on his buckskin shirt kept snagging on bushes. I motioned him forward, and he wriggled up beside me, keeping low. Together we parted the grass and peered down at the enemy camp.

It had been easy following the girls back. We'd stayed a safe distance behind them, keeping under cover and following their voices. They'd never suspected a thing.

"Two tents," I whispered. "One for the girls, I guess, and one for the aunt."

Pete nodded. "That should make it easy."

The girls weren't in sight, but we could hear their muffled voices, mixed with a lot of laughter, coming from inside one of the tents. We listened, but all I could catch were a few snatches of their conversation. Snatches like "moose," "duck," "moosey-woosey," "ducky-wucky," "hilarious," and "I thought I was going to die!"

I gritted my teeth and studied their camp.

The two tents were set up far apart, at either end of a large clearing by the lake. The big one at the far end was khaki colored and looked as if it had been on about a hundred African safaris. The canvas was scruffy and worn and was covered with all sorts of patches, but the tent itself was all shipshape and taut. It had a large canvas awning that stretched out from the front and was held up by two poles. In the shade of the awning were a small folding table with some books scattered on it, a canvas stool, and a tripod for a camera. The tent nearer to us was a modern one—a two-man A-frame made of red nylon. It was the one the girls' voices were coming from.

Between the tents, but set forward near the lake, was a stone fire ring with an iron grate. The shoreline was curved and rocky, with a tiny stretch of sand at the far end near the big safari tent. Two canoes were beached on the sandy spot. Also at the far end, tied between two trees, was a clothesline—with two T-shirts and a pair of white socks hung out to dry.

I was busy gauging the distance between the forest and the lake, when suddenly the girls came bursting out of their tent, still laughing. At us, of course. Pete and I must have been the best entertainment they'd had in years.

"Funny," muttered Pete in a low voice. "They think they're so f—"

"Lo!" cried the one named Jill, gesturing grandly at her friend. "It is I, Mighty Moose!"

"Behold!" replied Sunny, her arms thrown wide. "It is I, Dummy Duck!"

Pete made a choking sound and started over the hill. I grabbed his arm and pulled him back.

"Hear me, O Duck," said Jill. "Why are thy tennis shoes so wet and squishy?"

"Because, O Moose, I have fallen into the stormy sea! After all, they do not call me Dummy Duck for nothing!"

Naturally, they practically choked to death laughing over that one. Then they went on for a while longer, more or less in the same vein. Pete and I tried to stay calm, but it wasn't easy.

Finally they decided to take a break. Sunny

24

ducked inside their tent and came out with a wicker basket and a plaid blanket. She went over to the shade of a big rock near the lake, spread the blanket out, and began unpacking some food.

Jill, meanwhile, headed for the safari tent. She discovered a piece of paper under a rock on the folding table, looked at it for a minute, and then waved it in the air.

"Aunt Katherine left a note," she called across the clearing. "She decided to get an early start, since she has to set up her camera equipment. She says she'll be out all night, so we shouldn't wait up."

"What about the bird blind?" asked Sunny.

"She'll show us tomorrow."

Sunny nodded. "Want a sandwich?" she said, holding up a piece of bread.

"Sure," said Jill. "Be there in a minute." With a flick of her ponytail, she ducked inside the safari tent.

We'd heard enough. I nudged Pete and we inched back from the crest of the hill.

"So," whispered Pete meaningfully, "good old Aunt Katherine will be gone all night. Which means . . ."

I finished his thought: ". . . the coast'll be clear."

Grinning evilly, we slithered back down the hill.

5

An hour later, back at the cove, Pete staggered over to a tree and crumpled against it. He was a wreck. His T-shirt was torn and bloodied. Mud was spattered across his chest. His hair was tangled, his belt hung loose from two belt loops, and one of his shoes was missing.

"More blood," I told him. "You need a little more blood on your forehead."

I squashed some more berries, mixed the juice with a little Chuck's Extra-Thick Tomato Sauce, and smeared the gooey mess on his forehead. Then I stood back to admire my work.

26

Pete grinned. "How do I look?" he asked.

I mashed a fistful of mud on his left shoulder. "Horrible," I said proudly. "Really horrible. In fact, I think I'm going to be sick."

We were making our way back to the girls' camp when suddenly we heard their voices ahead of us on the trail. Quickly, we ducked off the trail, circled around closer, and checked out the situation.

Jill was down on her knees, pouring some white stuff on the ground. It took me a few seconds to figure out what she was doing. She was making a plaster cast of an animal track—I knew because I'd read an article about how to do it and had always wanted to try it myself.

Sunny, meanwhile, was standing there with her arms crossed in front of her and her weight on one foot, telling Jill all about a book she was reading called *Famous Stuntwomen of Hollywood*. She was saying how one of the women in the book was especially good at jumping onto things—like moving trains and stagecoaches and stuff like that. And another woman specialized in falling off things—like buildings and cliffs and so forth.

Actually, it was all pretty interesting, and I could tell from Pete's expression that he would've liked to stick around and hear more, but we had a job

27

to do. And we had to do it now, before Pete's blood dried up and began looking like tomato sauce.

I nudged him and we melted back into the forest, circled back around to the trail, and started toward the girls.

By the time they saw us, Pete was limping along beside me, clutching my arm for support. There was a dazed expression on his face. "Those claws . . ." he was babbling hoarsely. "Those horrible claws . . ."

I heard the girls gasp. Sunny stood frozen, her mouth open. Jill, rising slowly to her feet, dropped her bucket of plaster on the ground, and white liquid poured out over the trail.

"Don't worry, Pete," I was saying soothingly. "It's over now. You're going to be all right."

"What *happened*?" blurted Sunny. She was gaping at Pete's torn shirt and bloody wounds, looking horrified. Jill's expression was harder to read, but I thought she looked pretty upset, too.

Pete moaned.

"It's nothing," I told them. "He's okay. He's just scratched up a little. He was attacked by a wolverine."

"A *what*?" said Jill, shifting her piercing blue eyes to me.

"A wolverine. A really big one. He—"

"**DON'T LET HIM GET ME!**" screamed Pete. Shielding his face with his hands, he began to topple over backward. I caught him just in time.

"It jumped on him from a tree," I explained. "But I have to give Pete credit. He put up a good fight. He fought like a lion."

The bit about the lion was Pete's idea. I felt pretty silly saying it, but he'd made me promise to work it in somehow. At least it was better than saying that he'd fought like a dozen wild Tasmanian devils, which is what he'd really wanted me to say. I'd told him to forget it.

Pete's eyes were wandering aimlessly, focusing on nothing. His head rolled slowly in a sort of circle.

"What's a wolverine?" Sunny asked, nervously twisting her long blond hair with her fingers. She'd hardly taken her eyes off Pete. "I've never even heard of one."

I'd been counting on that, because I hardly knew anything about wolverines myself. All I knew was that they are about four feet long, that they look a little like small bears, that they are fierce fighters, and that they can kill animals much larger than themselves.

"They're about four feet long," I said, "and

they look a little like small bears. They are very fierce fighters, and they can kill animals much larger than themselves."

So much for the facts. Now for the fantasy.

"Actually," I went on, "I think this may have been one of your North American vampire wolverines, because of the way it went for Pete's neck."

That shook them up—even Jill. She looked a little white. "Of course," I added, "they don't actually suck blood. It's just that they always kill by going for the soft underside of the neck."

Heh, heh. This was kind of fun. And *tonight*, I thought to myself gleefully, was going to be even more fun.

A bit of berry juice and tomato sauce oozed down the side of Pete's face and dripped onto his shirt.

"Doesn't he need a doctor?" Jill asked me.

Pete began to come out of his daze. He lolled his head in Jill's direction and crossed his eyes. "Doctor?" he said weakly.

"I think a little first aid should do it," I said, trying to sound like someone who stays cool in an emergency. "I'm going to take Pete over to the mainland and see if I can get some help at the lodge. I just came by to find you, so I could warn you about the wolverine before we left."

"You think it'll attack again?" Sunny asked in a worried voice.

I shrugged. "You know how it is. Once a wild animal has tasted human blood, he's never the same again. But I wouldn't worry about it if I were you. It's a big island, and I doubt if he'll be able to find you."

I let that sink in for a few seconds. While I did, a bird suddenly made a fluttering sound in a nearby bush. Jill and Sunny practically jumped out of their tennis shoes.

Mission accomplished, I thought. The groundwork had been laid, and it was time to be moving on.

"Well, I'll be seeing you," I said casually. "Pete and I'd better get moving if we're going to get to the lodge before dark."

I patted Pete tenderly on his shoulder and then took his arm.

"Ready, old buddy?" I asked him.

He perked up. "Go bye-bye?" he asked cheerfully.

I turned him around and led him gently away.

"We did it!" whooped Pete. "They were scared, really scared."

"But not as scared as they're going to be," I said in high spirits.

Pete did a spooky version of his whistling-wind sound effect. Then, making his voice low and quavery, he said, "As darkness falls over Turtle Island, the dreaded vampire wolverine begins to prowl." He snickered wickedly. "They'll run screaming right into the lake."

I grinned.

"We can only hope," I said.

6

The next order of business was the little matter of where to pitch our tent. Naturally we were going to have to be very careful. It went without saying that if the girls ever caught us living in a Hänsel and Gretel's Gingerbread House Tent, with candy canes and sugarplums all over the place, we'd have to hide out for the rest of our lives.

What we needed, Pete and I agreed, was a totally secret place to set up the tent, a place *nobody* could ever find. And we needed it in a hurry, too. Big black thunderheads were building up in the sky to the north. A storm was coming, and we were going to need shelter quick.

We loaded all our stuff in the canoe, and within minutes we were paddling along the west side of the island, hugging the shore, keeping our eyes peeled for a possible hideout. Whenever we saw a good landing place, we pulled in and did some quick exploring on foot.

About a quarter mile north of our starting point, on our fourth stop, we hit pay dirt. We stumbled onto the world's best hiding place.

It was perfect. So perfect we never would have found it if we hadn't gotten lost. From our canoe we'd spotted what looked like a cave on the side of a low hill. We beached our canoe and hiked inland to check it out. It turned out to be only a shallow opening under a rock outcropping, so we started back and that's when we got lost.

When we finally came out near the shore, it was at a place where an enormous rock, twenty or thirty feet high and about sixty feet wide, jutted into the lake. As we were pushing our way through the underbrush at the base of the rock, Pete happened to notice a long, narrow shelf, bending around the left side of the rock. It was barely above water level. We investigated and found that there was just enough room, if we turned sideways, to squeeze by without slipping into the water.

"Me, Pathfinder," said Pete, leading the way.

On the back side of the rock, cut off from the rest of the island, we found our new home—a small, flat promontory with a cozy little clearing right in the middle of it. All around the edge of the promontory was a thick growth of trees and underbrush, so that the clearing itself was almost entirely hidden from anyone who might canoe by on the lake. All we'd have to do was plug up a few holes here and there with dead branches and we'd have complete privacy.

We were both pretty excited, and right away Pete named the promontory Hidden Valley.

"But it's not a valley," I pointed out.

"Yeah, but it has a good ring to it," he said. "And anyway, it'll confuse the enemy in case they ever overhear us talking about it."

I couldn't argue with that. Besides, now that we'd found a campsite, we had to move fast. The thunderstorm was closing in. The sky had turned a dark gray, and the temperature was dropping. The wind gusted across the lake.

First we found our canoe, paddled it to the promontory, and dragged it up into the trees so it couldn't be seen. Then we unpacked our Tiny

Tot Tent for Backyard Camping and hurriedly began setting it up in the clearing.

Just across the lake, jagged bolts of lightning were flashing out of the gray clouds. I measured the time between one of the flashes and the loud clap of thunder that followed. Two seconds—which meant the lightning was less than half a mile away. Close.

By the time we finished pitching the tent and rolling out the plastic cobblestone sidewalk with the tulips alongside, the first raindrops had begun to fall—big bloopy drops that made a little splash when they hit you. We grabbed our gear, threw it inside and, just as the downpour really began, dived in ourselves.

So . . .

There we were . . .

Surrounded by the deluxe model of Hänsel and Gretel's Gingerbread House Tent.

For a minute Pete and I just stood there, letting our eyes adjust to the dim light. The rain beat down on the canvas roof, making a loud drumming sound. Finally Pete got out his flashlight and shined it on one of the walls.

There was the witch. Still there. Still goofy-looking. Smiling sweetly, offering us cupcakes.

Trying to ignore the tent seemed like the best course of action, so we waited out the storm by unpacking a couple of books, lounging against our rolled-up sleeping bags, and reading by flash-light. Pete started a book called *Escape to Terror River*, and I began a new chapter in my astronomy book, about the moons of Jupiter.

The storm was violent but short. As soon as it passed, Pete and I got back to work and finished setting up camp. Even though the sun had set, there was still a little light to work by.

Together we built a fire ring with stones we hauled up from the lakeshore. Then we gathered as much firewood as we could carry from the other side of the big rock. While we were there, we made sure to camouflage the entrance to the shelf leading to Hidden Valley.

"No human," Pete informed me, "could find us now."

We cooked a great dinner. Well, actually, I guess it wasn't really all that great. All it was was beans and Kool-Aid. But it *seemed* great, because we *felt* so great. There we were, on our own, cooking out under the stars on a warm August night. The sky had cleared and the Milky Way really stood out, streaming across the sky like a ghostly white river. Even Pete thought it was beautiful.

After dinner, our thoughts turned to the girls. And to our master plan. We weren't going into action until about midnight, so we had plenty of time to relax around the campfire, listening to the crickets, watching the fireflies, and ironing out the details of our plan of attack.

Ah, sweet revenge.

It was a dark and moonless night. Heh, heh. Just the sort of night that brings out the worst in a vampire wolverine.

7

"GRRUNH! GRRUNH! GRRUNH! GRRUNH! GRRUNH! GRRUNH!"

It was eleven o'clock—still an hour before the attack. Pete stood in the flickering light of our campfire. His face was red. His eyes were wild and gleaming. Heaving, gasping, he clawed the air with his hands.

"GRRUNH! GRRUNH! GRRUNH! GRR—"

"Hold it, hold it, hold it," I interrupted, shaking my head. "That's good, Pete. That's really good. But I think it sounds a little too much like a bear. It's got to be a wolverine. I tell you what.

See if you can add a little wild boar to it. That might help."

"Right," said Pete. He shut his eyes and took a few deep breaths, preparing himself. Neither of us had ever heard a wolverine before, but I knew I could count on Pete to come up with something convincing.

Pete's face took on a sort of snoutish appearance, so I knew he was thinking of a wild boar.

"You might add some wolf, too," I suggested. "A hungry one. Maybe with a disturbed mind."

Pete nodded, and I watched his face slowly change, his features twisting into those of a crazed and vicious beast. With lots of snout.

Suddenly he opened his mouth, and out came a long, horrible, ear-splitting howl that made my blood run cold. He followed that up with a series of savage, snuffling snarls and low snorts.

I was impressed.

"What do you think?" he asked. He tried to look modest, but he didn't succeed. Pete knows he's good at animal imitations. In fact, everybody in our whole school knows he's good. Last year Pete and I entered our school's Annual Radio Drama Contest, and when we read the play I'd written, called *Attack of the Killer Bees*, over the P.A. system, Pete really stole the show.

The story was about an attack by giant killer

bees on a jungle outpost, and Pete not only did your standard sound effects—like creaking doors and whistling wind—but also the sound effects for both the heroine's pet gorilla, Igor, and the evil head bee, Black Buzz. I'll never forget Pete's version of the final battle between Igor and Black Buzz. It was a masterpiece—two minutes of enraged snarls, howls, yips, grunts, and buzzes that kept the whole school on the edge of their seats. Just listening to him, I knew we'd win the contest hands down—and we did.

Pete's good, all right. And now he had come through again.

"Well?" he repeated. "How was it?"

"Let me put it this way," I told him with a grin. "It's definitely going to get their attention."

8

August 9, 2400 hours:

"Now!" I whisper to Pete, and we swoop down on them, out of the forest. It's midnight and they are asleep in their tent. We hit them with everything we've got. The attack is on!

Grunting, snarling, growling, Pete circles their tent at high speed, ferociously raking the sides of it with the artificial claws we made out of tree branches. *The wolverine wants in.*

Working fast, I remove the six stakes around the base of the tent, as well as the ones that anchor the ropes attached to the tent poles, front and back. I gather the freed ropes in my hands, like reins.

Pete cups his hands around his mouth and howls his head off. *The wolverine smells girl and wants to eat girl.*

I begin jerking rapidly on the ropes. The tent poles are dancing, the tent is swaying, the sides are billowing.

Not a peep from inside. Too scared even to scream.

Now Pete is working at the door, digging at it, reaching under it and clawing at the nylon floor. He is whining. *The wolverine cannot wait.*

I station myself at the front of the tent. I have the fake wolverine under one arm—Pete's torn T-shirt stuffed with leaves. Pete—snorting and snuffling—finds the zipper and in one quick motion unzips the front of their tent. He jumps aside, flinging open the tent flaps. I toss the wolverine inside, grab the camera hanging from around my neck, and aim it at the girls.

For the picture of a lifetime! For the picture of our dreams! For—

Wait.

Something's wrong.

The tent is empty.

"Oh, boys. Looking for someone?"

The girls are behind us! We spin around. I

43

take a bucket of water in the face. It's cold and it's got something slimy in it—water lilies, maybe, or some sort of gunk from the bottom of the lake.

Pete gets a bucketful, too. A lily pad gets caught on his ear.

"GET 'EM!" roars Pete.

Whooping with laughter, the girls gallop back across the clearing. Pete and I whip out our flashlights and sprint after them. I don't stop to ask myself what we're going to do if we catch them. I don't have any idea. But I definitely don't think we're going to ask them for their hands in marriage.

They skid around the safari tent and hightail it into the trees. Pete and I follow at full speed. We trip over the clothesline that is slung low, at ankle level, between two trees. We sprawl forward, belly-flopping into a soft pile of mud and leaves.

A flash goes off.

A camera flash.

They've done it again.

Covered with mud and bristling with leaves, we charged out into their clearing. We were after that camera and we meant business.

We saw too late that there was a woman standing in the middle of the clearing, a couple of cameras slung around her neck, her hands on her hips, squared off in front of Jill and Sunny in a no-nonsense stance.

"What's going on here?" she was demanding.

It didn't take a genius to figure out that it was Aunt Katherine, back early from her night photography. And she looked like a pretty tough customer.

She caught sight of us, and the three of them turned and looked at us. The girls shined their flashlights in our direction.

We dived back into the forest.

"Who were *they*?" we heard Aunt Katherine blurt out.

We didn't get more than five feet before I ran into a stiff little bush about waist high, bounced off, and smashed into Pete. We went down.

"Oh, *them*," Jill was explaining casually. "They're just a couple of North American vampire wolverines. But don't worry, Aunt Katherine. I don't think they'll be back."

9

We trudged home—discouraged, dejected, in the dumps. The commando team of Moose Mc-Kenzie and Duck Wilson had definitely fallen on hard times.

Pete stopped to kick a tree.

"Rats!" he said for the fiftieth time. "How could we be so *stupid*?"

"Because we're numbskulls," I explained glumly. "We're nitwits. We're a couple of North American nitwitted numbskulls."

We had our flashlights out and were following

46

an unfamiliar trail. We would have gone back the same way we came, but we'd made such a hasty exit from the girls' camp that we'd missed our turnoff. We weren't worried, though, because the trail we were on seemed to be headed for the big hill in the middle of the island. Earlier that day, just before dark, we'd taken a compass reading on the hill from a point near Hidden Valley, figuring that it was probably the highest point on the island and would make a good landmark. Now all we had to do was get to the top of the hill, use the opposite reading, and we should come out close to home. Already the trail was beginning to climb.

Behind me, Pete gave a snort of disbelief.

"Yeah, but how could we be so *stupid?*" he blurted.

I wiped some of the mud off my forehead. "You got me," I said grimly. "They just outsmarted us, that's all. They saw through us right from the start." I shook my head and then added meaningfully, "But *next* time . . ."

"Yeah," said Pete, still disgusted but with a little ray of hope in his voice. "Next time we won't be so *stupid.*"

It turned out that the trail did lead to the hilltop—or at least to the jumble of large boulders that covered the summit. Before heading down and to the west, Pete and I decided to climb to the top of the highest rock for a look around.

A minute later we were surveying the whole of Turtle Island. Since there was no moon and it was a dark night, the island itself was inky black, but it was silhouetted clearly against the dark gray of the lake. Overhead, a couple of bats swooped after insects. The sky was full of hundreds of stars. Just out of habit, I located the North Star and some of the brightest summer stars—Vega, Deneb, and Altair.

We looked southeast, in the direction of the girls' camp. No lights. Which was logical, since their campsite was probably hidden by trees. And besides, they were probably sound asleep by now— with big happy grins on their faces, merrily chuckling away. The creeps.

I checked out the north. Most of the island lay in that direction, stretching out for three quarters of a mile or more before coming to a point. For us it was all unexplored territory.

Suddenly, I saw something.

Something weird.

In the distance, against the blackness of the island, almost at the northern tip, an eerie orange light was moving. "Pete, look!" I said.

48

For four or five seconds the light moved to the left, traveling fast. Much faster than a person could run. Then it paused and moved quickly back to the right. It looked like it might be flying, but the pattern didn't make sense. It moved to the left again, then to the right—slowing down slightly, cutting its distance each time, almost as if it were zeroing in on one particular spot. Left, right, left, right. Then, suddenly, it moved in a perpendicular direction for a short distance, as if it were dropping to the ground—and was gone.

It disappeared. Completely.

We stood there staring tensely into the darkness, waiting for the light to reappear. But it didn't.

Finally Pete spoke. "Spooky. What do you think it was, Scott?"

"I don't know," I said. "But one thing's for sure. There's someone else on the island."

"Or some*thing* else."

"Yeah," I said. I tried to think of a logical explanation but couldn't come up with one. "I say we hike over there first thing in the morning and find out what's going on."

We started climbing down the boulders, heading for home.

"It's probably more girls," said Pete gloomily.

"They're probably flying them in by helicopter now. Pretty soon the island will be full of them."

By the time we arrived back at Hidden Valley we were pretty worn out. It had been a long day— a long *hard* day. We'd canoed across a lot of water; we'd fallen in a lot of water; we'd hiked across a lot of land; we'd fallen in a lot of mud. We needed sleep and lots of it.

Right away Pete tripped over one of the tulips along the plastic sidewalk in front of our Gingerbread Tent.

"Rotten tulips," he grumped. "I wish I had a lawn mower. I'd *mow* those tulips."

We would have slept out under the stars, but we thought there was a good chance it would rain again before morning. So we got out of our muddy clothes, took a quick dip in the lake to clean off, spread out our sleeping bags inside the tent, and climbed into them.

I took a few minutes to wipe the mud off my camera and see if it still worked. I looked through the viewfinder, took a flash picture of the witch on the wall, and advanced the film. Everything seemed okay.

"We'll get the girls tomorrow," I told Pete. "We'll work out a plan. Something good."

"It'd better be better than our last plan," said

Pete. "You could grind up our last plan and use it as chicken feed."

"Don't worry. They're smarter than we thought, but they can be beaten. This time we'll use our wits. We'll outthink them."

"Just as long as we cream them," said Pete.

"Trust me," I said. I put my camera aside and turned off my flashlight.

As I lay there, I found myself thinking about Jill. I was sure she was the one who'd seen through us. I remembered the way she'd looked at me—with those probing blue eyes of hers—when I'd told about how Pete had been attacked by the wolverine. Yeah, it was her, all right. It had to be.

I was just drifting off to sleep when I felt Pete jabbing me.

"What's *that*?" he said.

"What's what?"

"Up there. On the ceiling."

I looked up. Glowing dimly on the ceiling of the tent were some tiny, tiny letters. They must have been painted on with phosphorescent paint. I couldn't quite make them out, so I sat up and squinted at them. Slowly, I read them out loud.

Upsy-daisy in the morning!
Downsy-snoozy in the night!

51

"That's really sickening," said Pete with disgust. "I think I'm going to upsy-daisy my dinner."

I fluffed up the jacket I was using as a pillow and flopped back down on it.

"Take it easy, Pete," I said soothingly. "Downsy-snoozy. Downsy-snoozy."

10

Early the next morning we were up, out, and on
our way—heading north, searching for the source
of the mysterious light we'd seen the night before.
We figured we'd take care of the girls later. They
could wait. "Let 'em stew," said Pete. Of course,
what he really meant was that we hadn't thought
of a decent plan yet.

We worked our way along the shore on foot,
passing a large, shallow cove with a lot of frogs
and turtles sitting around on rocks. Pete named
it Bullfrog Lagoon. Then we cut inland and picked
up a trail. We were almost to the tip of the is-

land—somewhere close to where the light must have come from—when we heard the cry.

It was a Tarzan yell. A terrific one—echoing through the forest, deep and powerful. My spine tingled. It was absolutely and positively the best Tarzan yell I'd ever heard outside the movies. I mean it. It could have been the Lord of the Jungle himself.

Seconds after it died away, we heard a loud splash.

And then nothing.

Pete gave me a questioning look, but I just shrugged. The only explanation I could think of wasn't worth mentioning: that Tarzan had just dived into the water to rescue Jane and was wrestling with the crocodile.

I motioned to Pete and we moved ahead, slowly and cautiously now. The trees were gigantic in this part of the island, towering over us and casting cool, deep shadows. The forest floor was soft and springy. Just right for good sneaking.

After about fifty yards, the trail suddenly ended at the lake. Or rather, it ended at the head of a long, narrow inlet of the lake, with huge trees crowding right up to the shore on both sides. Pete and I hung back among the shadows, sort of sizing things up.

There wasn't anybody in the water at the moment, but there definitely had been, and recently too. Because hanging directly above the middle of the inlet was a long, thick rope. Still swaying.

I looked up. The rope itself wasn't hanging from a tree branch because there weren't any branches that reached that far out over the water. Instead, it was suspended from the middle of another rope that had been tied between the tops of two tall trees on opposite sides of the inlet.

Something else caught my eye. On the right side of the inlet, about twenty feet up in one of the trees, was a wooden platform built out over the water. It was obviously the jump-off point for a long rope swing across the inlet.

"Boy, neat!" I said to Pete in a low voice.

I leaned around the tree for a look at the other side of the inlet, thinking there might be another platform opposite the first one.

There was. But there was a lot more besides.

I froze, staring. Pete must have seen it, too, because I heard him gasp. "Wow!" he whispered.

There, high in the leafy branches of three enormous trees, was a tree house. A fantastic tree house. A tree house with small rooms perched far out on strong branches and larger rooms, with balconies, built back among the leaves. With long rope ladders hanging to the ground, and stairways that spiraled around tree trunks and out onto branches, ending in small platforms with sturdy railings and benches for sitting. There were storage barrels and big wooden flowerpots and old-fashioned brass lanterns hanging from tree limbs. There were wood buckets on ropes, attached to pulleys, for drawing water up from the lake. And connecting the three trees were long suspension bridges with wood plank floors and rope railings.

Suddenly, a voice behind us said, "I think I've just about got the hang of it!"—and Pete and I jumped about a foot in the air.

When we came down, we spun around and found ourselves face to face with a pleasant-looking, middle-aged man with a friendly, intelligent face, thinning hair, and a little too much weight around the middle. He was wearing faded cutoffs and beat-up old tennis shoes that were coming apart at the toes. He was dripping wet.

He gestured to the rope hanging over the inlet. "I almost made it that time," he said cheerfully. He gave us the thumbs-up sign. "Looking good, looking good."

I wasn't sure what to say. "Uh," I began politely, "you were trying to swing from one platform to the other?"

"That's right," he said. He did four or five

jumping jacks. "I've been working at it for a week now, and this was the closest I've come so far. I think it was my Tarzan yell. It really got my adrenaline going."

"It was a great yell," offered Pete. He meant it. Pete does a pretty good Tarzan yell himself.

"Oh, do you really think so?" said the man, looking pleased.

"Yeah, I really do," said Pete. "It was first-rate."

"I used to practice it in the shower," said the man modestly, "but I never knew it would come in handy. It almost did the trick, though. Did you see me?"

"No, we missed it," I said. "We were back there in the woods."

"Well, first I gave my yell, and then I gave this terrific push-off. I was really moving. When I got to the other side, I got both feet on the platform, but I was off balance and I couldn't quite let go of the rope and grab the hand pole. Before I knew it, I was swinging back the other way." He gave a little shrug. "It was all over then, of course. I swung back and forth until I couldn't hold on any longer, and then took the big plunge into the lake."

Suddenly I had an idea.

"I don't suppose you were swinging on your

rope last night, were you?" I asked him. "About twelve-thirty or one o'clock?"

He looked surprised. "I sure was. How'd you know?"

I told him about Pete and me seeing the mysterious light and how it had moved back and forth and then disappeared.

"That was me, all right," he said. "Me and my trusty lantern. I'd been up on my moon-viewing platform."

"Your what?" I said.

"My moon-viewing platform." He pointed to the top of the huge tree on the right side of the inlet, across from the tree house. High up, much higher than the rope-swinging platform, almost at the very top of the tree, I could see a small, round platform. "I use it to contemplate the moon. But since there wasn't any moon last night, I was up there with my star map, trying to learn the constellations."

I couldn't believe it. A *moon-viewing* platform. I was beginning to like this guy better and better.

"It was a beautiful night," he went on, "and when I came down I was feeling so good I absolutely *knew* I could swing across the inlet. So I hooked my lantern over my arm, grabbed the rope, and let 'er rip."

He sighed. Then, shaking his head sadly, he

leaned forward and peered into the deep water of the inlet.

"I survived," he said solemnly, "but my lantern didn't. Poor thing, it went to a watery grave."

11

"Did you know," Cornelius asked us, "that we're not alone on the island? There's a fascinating woman camping somewhere about. And two charming girls, too, just about your age."

Pete choked.

"Oh?" I managed to say. "Two girls?"

The man's name had turned out to be Cornelius Callihan, and we were midway through a tour of his tree house. He'd been coming to Turtle Island for three summers, he said, and each summer he'd added a little more—a room here, a bridge there, an almost-impossible rope swing way over there.

He'd taken us on a roundabout route, "just to make things more interesting." First we'd climbed up a long rope ladder into the left-hand tree and gone out a short causeway to the library—a sunny room with bookshelves all around, a cuckoo clock on the wall, a comfortable reading chair, and a solid-oak footstool. Then it was up some winding steps to his workshop—cluttered with coils of rope, cans of nails, odds and ends of wood, lots of tools hanging on the walls, and several ongoing projects.

After that we went up another ladder, ducked around the tree, went out on a branch to a sitting platform, and then crossed a long, narrow suspension bridge to the middle tree. We were above the living room and breakfast balcony now, so we left them for later and climbed even higher to his bedroom, a small room with an old leather trunk at the foot of the bed, a bright-red rug on the floor, and a hand-carved birdhouse hanging just outside the window.

And now, after crossing another long, swaying bridge, we were taking a short rest on a sitting platform high in the third tree.

"That's right," said Cornelius, "two girls. They

said their names were Jill and Sunny. I met them just this morning. Do you know them?"

Honesty is almost always the best policy, so I probably should have come right out and admitted everything. I probably should have looked him in the eye, man to man, and said, "Sure, we know them. They're our sworn enemies. In fact, we carried out a midnight raid on their camp last night, but we made a few tactical mistakes while we were there, and we'd really rather not talk about it if you don't mind."

But instead I stammered, "Yeah, well, uh, sort of. I mean, I guess you could say we've *met* them, but we don't really *know* them. I mean, we *have* talked to them a little bit, but we're not best friends or anything."

"Well, you might want to get to know them better," said Cornelius firmly. "They're two of the nicest young ladies I've met in a long time."

Pete made a kind of gurgling noise.

"And Katherine!" exclaimed Cornelius, his eyes suddenly lighting up. "Katherine is Jill's aunt, you know. What an extraordinary woman! A woman of character and intelligence. A woman of spirit!" He paused, gazing dreamily out over the forest. "You should have seen her eyes flash when she told me I was an idiot."

He looked delighted.

I didn't exactly know what to say, so I just sort of smiled politely. But Pete, as usual, got right to the point. "She called you an idiot?" he asked, looking interested.

"She did," said Cornelius, beaming fondly at the memory. "And she was entirely within her rights, too. I deserved everything she said. After all, I knocked over her tripod, squashed her camera case, and broke her tree."

Pete and I stared at him.

"You attacked her camp?" said Pete, amazed.

Cornelius looked puzzled. "Attacked her camp? Why, no. Why would I want to do that?"

"Oh, uh, no reason," said Pete, backpedaling. He began fiddling with the fringe on his buckskin shirt. "It was just a thought."

"I don't even know where her camp is," said Cornelius. "I only met her this morning, on my early-morning hike." He sighed, remembering. "There she was, as I came around a tree, kneeling in the soft morning light, cinching up the shoelaces on her hiking boots."

For a moment Cornelius seemed lost in wonder.

"It was such a lovely vision," he went on, "that I forgot to watch where I was going, and before I knew it I'd run smack into her tripod. It started to fall over and when I tried to stop it, I tripped

63

over it, became somewhat entangled in the thing, and went down—landing, unfortunately, on her aluminum camera case. But the worst part was that as I was falling, I reached out and grabbed hold of the tree trunk that was standing next to me. It turned out not to be a real tree trunk at all, but the fake one that Katherine hides inside when she takes pictures of birds. It was made of cardboard or papier-mâché or something, and I'm afraid I rather destroyed it."

"I guess that's when she called you an idiot," volunteered Pete.

"Exactly," said Cornelius. "She called me a blithering idiot, a clumsy oaf, and a general, all-around menace." His eyes sparkled. "What a woman!" he said.

Pete and I exchanged a look.

"Of course," he continued, "I felt it was wise to cut my visit short after that, and it was on my way back that I met Jill and Sunny. Naturally, I asked them all about Katherine. Did you know she's a professional wildlife photographer? A darn good one, too, I'll bet. By the way, have you met her?"

I shrugged my shoulders and tried to look casual. "Briefly," I said. "Very, very briefly. I don't even think she'd recognize us if she saw us again."

How could she? The only time she saw us was

at night, and we were wearing a thick coat of mud and leaves from head to toe.

"Say, Cornelius, what's that room down there?" said Pete, trying to change the subject.

"Oh, that," said Cornelius. "That's my writing room." He got up. "Come on, I'll show you."

We climbed down and went into a small room built across two strong branches at the back of the tree. It was open and airy, with windows all around. In fact, the entire top half of the front wall was completely open, with rolled-up canvas to let down in case of rain. Outside, mostly what you saw were leaves, with soft sunlight filtering through them, so that the room had a secret, hidden feeling to it.

In the middle of the floor, on a faded red-and-gray Indian rug, was a table with an old typewriter and a messy pile of papers on it. There were stacks of books on the floor, an enormous dictionary on a special stand all by itself, and some watercolor paintings of birds on the walls.

"What kind of stuff do you write?" I asked.

"Detective novels," replied Cornelius. "I've written eight Max Malone mysteries and I'm working on my ninth now."

"Wow," I said. "I've never met a real writer before."

"Hey, is this one of yours?" asked Pete.

He was holding up a paperback called *The Buddha Bleeds at Midnight*, by C. P. Callihan. The picture on the front showed a man with flinty eyes and a trench coat effortlessly blocking a punch thrown by some guy wearing a karate outfit. In the background were a lot of neon signs in Japanese and a scene of an old man sitting on a mat floor, staring at a golden Buddha. Across the bottom it said, "Another mystery-thriller with Max Malone—the thinking man's private eye."

Cornelius nodded. "That's my latest," he said. "I had a lot of fun with that one."

"How'd you decide to write mysteries?" I asked him.

"Oh, I don't know," he said. "I guess it's because I've always loved adventure—in theory, anyway. Can't say that I've really had many adventures myself. It seems like I've spent most of my time at home in front of my typewriter, thinking up exciting things for Max Malone to do. In fact, one of the reasons I built this tree house," he said, looking around with satisfaction, "was that I decided it was about time for me to have a few adventures of my own."

Pete flipped through the book. "This looks great," he said. "Do you mind if we borrow it?"

"Not at all," said Cornelius. "You can keep it if you like. I have lots more."

He asked us if we wanted to have a snack down on his breakfast balcony, overlooking the inlet. We said yes, but just as we were heading out the door, I happened to glance back at the typewriter—and suddenly an idea popped into my head.

A terrific idea. A brilliant idea.

An idea for how to put a certain pair of giggling girls in their places.

I stopped. "Say, Cornelius," I said, "would it be okay if Pete and I used your typewriter a little later? There's something important we'd like to type."

"Sure," he said. "In fact, you can use it right now if you want. You could join me below when you're finished."

Pete looked confused, but I hurried on before he had a chance to say anything. "Gee, thanks, Cornelius. That'd be great."

"There's plenty of typing paper on the table," Cornelius said. "Take your time. I'll just be tidying up a bit. After all, it's always possible Katherine might happen by." He started down the ladder, humming to himself.

I pulled Pete back inside. "What's going on?" he wanted to know.

I explained my plan.

He liked it. He liked it a lot. He said the girls

were finished. He said they were goners. He said the hour was at hand when the two of us could once again hold up our heads with pride. When we could once again walk tall among the cool shadows of the deep dark forest. He said I was a genius. He said I was—

"*Pete!*"

—a wonderful and fantastic genius and that I could have his hunting horn, his buckskin shirt, and his very life if need be. He said—

"**PETE**!"

"Mmm?"

"Can we just write the letter?"

"Right."

We got down to business. First we worked out a few details, and then I sat down at the typewriter, put in a clean sheet of paper, and began typing.

Half an hour later we were finished. I pulled the sheet out with a flourish, and we read it again, snickering to ourselves.

"And now," I said gleefully as I folded the letter and put it in my pocket, "all we have to do is go back to Bullfrog Lagoon and catch a couple of turtles."

12

We had our turtles and we were ready.

Three hours had passed. A busy three hours. We'd had our snack with Cornelius (Fig Newtons and lemonade), we'd tried out the rope swing (and failed—it *was* impossible), we'd agreed to come back that night (for some stargazing on Cornelius's moon-viewing platform), we'd stopped at Bullfrog Lagoon (bagging two big turtles in five minutes flat), we'd dropped by our Gingerbread House (for some fishing line and a couple of plastic Ziploc sandwich bags), and we were now in position at the girls' camp.

Pete stood ready at the edge of the forest, watching for my signal. Turtle One was under his arm. Turtle Two was with me, up on the crest of the hill overlooking the camp.

There was no one in sight, but Pete and I were in no hurry. We could wait.

Ten minutes passed . . . twenty . . .

There was a cricket somewhere in the bushes nearby, so I passed a little time by trying to figure out what the temperature was. I remembered reading in a nature book that all you have to do is count the number of cricket chirps in fifteen seconds and then add forty. If that was true, then it was 85 degrees Fahrenheit. Pretty hot. Of course, I already *knew* it was hot, but—

Suddenly, I spotted Jill and Sunny gliding around the point in their canoe. They were paddling hard, but there were still some trees between them and the clearing. Pete could make it if he was fast.

I signaled frantically, and Pete went into action. He raced out to the middle of the clearing, put Turtle One down on the ground, and sprinted back toward the trees, barely reaching cover before the girls cleared the point.

Keeping low, I quickly worked my way down the hill and joined Pete behind some bushes, where we had a good view of the clearing.

Right away we saw a flaw in our plan. We should've picked a slower turtle.

Turtle One turned out to be some kind of crazy speed demon. He was up on his tiptoes, practically galloping toward the forest on a line that would take him past the safari tent. He was a third of the way there already.

Pete and I squirmed. If Turtle One disappeared into the underbrush before the girls saw him, we'd be down and out. Back to square one.

As for Jill and Sunny, they were taking their time, carefully unloading their canoe, item by item. They'd been on a picnic or something, and they must have taken half their camp with them.

Turtle One was cruising along in high gear. No pain, no strain. *He* wasn't wasting any time.

Meanwhile, what the girls were mainly doing was talk, talk, talking. They talked about the raccoon they'd seen scurrying along the shore. They exclaimed about the rock they'd found with some kind of fossil in it. Jill talked about eyes. She said she liked brown eyes. She thought they were cute. They chatted about movie stunts. Sunny said she'd like to be a stuntwoman in a sword-and-sorcery movie, so she could do things like leap off castle walls.

Turtle One had his head down and was pouring on the steam. Pete groaned quietly.

71

Now the girls were bent over the canoe, looking for something they'd lost. I couldn't stand it. "Forget it!" I wanted to yell. "You can buy another one!"

Turtle One was in the homestretch, nearing the edge of the clearing. Our gooses were almost cooked.

Turtle One stopped!

And here came the girls! Up into the clearing, their arms full of picnic stuff. Turtle One was straight ahead of them. All they had to do was *look*.

The girls veered off in the direction of their tent. "No!" I croaked under my breath.

Just then Turtle One started up again. He only had two feet to go.

"Hey, look!" said Jill. "A turtle!" She must have seen him out of the corner of her eye. "And he's got something on his back!"

They threw down their stuff, ran over, and picked up Turtle One just as he was about to crawl under a bush.

Pete and I gave quiet sighs of relief.

Sunny held the turtle while Jill quickly untied the fishing line that held the plastic sandwich bag in place. "What's this?" said Jill, opening the bag and taking out our letter.

Sunny looked excited. "It's a letter!" she said.

They read it, Sunny looking over Jill's shoulder.

Abigail Peters III
5 Old Nob Road
Beacon Hill
Boston, Mass.
April 12, 1986

Dear Whoever You Are:
Oh, thank you, thank you, thank
you!!! You've found my precious little
Snowball. Isn't he absolutely the cutest
little turtle-kins you've ever seen? How
can I ever thank you??? Never mind—I know
how. Money, money, money! Now don't you
worry, I can afford it. People may say I'm
just an eccentric old lady, but at least
I'm a rich eccentric old lady. And I
certainly know what I can afford, you can
be quite sure about that.
As for Snowball, please leave him
where you found him. I only want you to
tell me that he's all right. You cannot
know how difficult it is for me to release
him into the wilderness (which I shall do
this very afternoon) after the many
wonderful years we have spent together.
But I can sense that the little darling is
not happy living in a luxurious mansion
in the middle of a big city. He longs to
have the fresh green grass tickling his
tiny toes. He was born free and he shall
live free!
Now, all you have to do is find
Snowball's charming little wife,
Poopsie. Finding her should be easy as

73

pie, since she and Snowball are never far apart. They are quite devoted to each other, you know.

So, quick as you can, find Poopsie, take the note from her back, send that note (together with this one) to me at the above address, and I'll have my private secretary send you some cold, hard cash. Let's make it five hundred dollars, shall we?

Are they all right? Do they look well? You can tell if Snowball is happy, because when he is happy, he will shake hands with you if you say, ''Put 'er there, pardner!'' He is a very clever turtle. Poopsie, on the other hand, is quite shy—but she's loads of fun once you get to know her.

Well, enough of my silly chatter! Just send me the letters—and a word or two about Snowball and Poopsie—and I'll send you the five hundred smackers.

Hugs and kisses to you. And please give my darling turtles some hugs and kisses too.

Very truly yours,

Abigail Peters III

Abigail Peters III

13

"It's got to be those guys," said Jill doubtfully. "Doesn't it? I mean, who ever heard of a five-hundred-dollar reward just for sending someone some news about a couple of turtles?"

"Put 'er there, pardner!" cried Sunny. She was lying on her stomach, her blond hair hooked behind her ears, and was offering her hand to Turtle One, now known as Snowball.

"A turtle can't shake hands," said Jill. "How can a turtle shake hands? It's probably got a brain the size of a pea."

Sunny was practically nose to nose with Snowball. "I think he's smiling," she said.

Jill leaned down and peered at the turtle. "How can you tell?"

"See the way his mouth turns up at the sides?"

Jill got down on her hands and knees and studied Snowball carefully. Finally she said, "It does sort of look like a smile." She held out her hand. "Put 'er there, pardner!" she said heartily. She had a great accent, right out of an old Western movie. She sounded just like Buffalo Bill greeting his old buddy Wild Bill Hickok.

Pete and I were trying our best not to make any noise—but it isn't easy to laugh your head off while not making a sound. If anyone said "Put 'er there, pardner!" one more time, we were going to be in real trouble.

"Poor baby," cooed Sunny, stroking Snowball's back. "He must be nervous. Aren't you, little turtle-kins?"

Pete let out a low, strangled squeak, and I quickly clapped my hand over his mouth.

Jill sat back on her heels and examined the Ziploc sandwich bag. Then she looked at the letter again.

"The letter's dated April twelfth," she pointed out. "That's four months ago. Does this bag look like it's been on a turtle's back for four months?"

76

You bet it did. Pete and I had given the bag the full treatment. We'd jumped up and down on it. We'd ground it into the dirt under our heels. We'd pounded it with a rock. That bag looked four months old if it looked a day.

"It looks pretty beat up to me," said Sunny.

There, you see?

Sunny got to her feet and picked up Snowball. "Let's find Poopsie," she said, looking eagerly around the clearing. "She must be around here somewhere."

Pete jabbed me in the side with his elbow. *"Poopsie!"* he mouthed silently. We almost collapsed.

Jill stood up. She still looked in doubt—but only a little. "I don't know," she said slowly. "I suppose the letter *must* be real. It's typewritten, and I don't see how the guys could possibly have a typewriter with them. I mean, they may be goofy, but they aren't stupid. Why would they lug a type-writer along on a camping trip?"

Goofy? Who was goofy?

"Yeah," said Sunny. "Besides, it just *sounds* real to me. I know a lot of people who're crazy about their pets. I know I am about my dog, Clyde."

"Well, maybe you're right. . . . I mean, just think. *Five hundred dollars!* . . . Wow!"

They made a quick sweep of the clearing. No

turtle. Then they started beating the bushes near where they'd caught Snowball, working their way slowly into the forest until they were out of sight.

Jill had been hard to convince, all right. If we'd written the letter by hand, she never would've bought it. Sunny seemed gung ho and ready to fall for anything, but Jill was a thinker. Now I was surer than ever that she was the one who'd caught on to our wolverine scam the day before.

So naturally it was music to my ears to hear Jill's voice ringing out through the forest, calling:

"Pooooooopsie! Oh, Poooooooooooopsie!"

I don't think Pete and I'd ever enjoyed ourselves so much in our lives.

Twenty minutes later Jill and Sunny gave up, and we could hear them returning to camp. Turtle Two was waiting for them. I'd planted him in the middle of the clearing, just about where Pete had put Turtle One.

This time we were lucky. Turtle Two was a very laid-back turtle. At the rate he was waddling along, it would take him a couple of months to reach the forest.

Jill and Sunny stepped into the clearing and spotted Turtle Two.

"Poopsie!" cried Jill, as if she were greeting a long-lost sister.

"Poopsie!" cried Sunny.

They charged over to Turtle Two, snapped him up, removed the plastic bag from his back, and put him and Turtle One down on the ground. Then they tore open the bag and leaned over the letter, grinning eagerly.

It was handwritten this time. And much shorter. It said:

Dear girls,
     Congratulations! You've found Poopsie. Now for your next assignment, see if you can find the whereabouts of your brains!

                    Your friends,
                    Moose and Duck

14

Naturally, the girls were a bit miffed.

And their mood hadn't improved any when Pete popped out from behind the bushes and yelled, "Hey, girls! Found those brains yet?" They'd stormed off to their tent with clenched fists, muttering darkly.

That made it easy for Pete and me to stroll out into the clearing and get Snowball and Poopsie. We took them back to Bullfrog Lagoon and set them loose. They'd done a good job, and we were a little sad to part with them.

"*Adiós*, pardners," said Pete fondly, giving them a big wave. "*Huevos rancheros!*"

"*Huevos rancheros?*" I said. "Pete, that's a type of eggs."

"Oh. I thought it meant 'good luck.'"

After we left Bullfrog Lagoon, we took the rest of the day off. We declared a holiday. The first thing we did was go back to Hidden Valley and roast some marshmallows. It seemed like the perfect way to celebrate, roasting marshmallows in the middle of the day.

After that we went swimming, floating on our backs, grinning up at the sky.

Then we lounged around awhile, chuckling a lot.

Finally, we got out Cornelius's book, *The Buddha Bleeds at Midnight*, and started reading it out loud. It was great. By the end of Chapter 4, the detective, Max Malone, really had his hands full. He'd only been on the case for three hours and already he'd found out plenty. Like that the parrot knew, but the parrot wouldn't talk. And that the chief of police had a theory, but the chief of police was missing. And that the computer had the answer, but the computer had self-destructed. We would've kept reading right on through to the end, but it started getting late and we had to fix dinner.

All in all, it had been a terrific day.

There was only one thing that kept sort of bothering me.

It was nothing, really. I don't even know why I was thinking about it. It was ridiculous. But for some reason I just kept wondering what Jill had meant, as she was unloading their canoe, when she said, "I like brown eyes. I think they're cute."

Whose brown eyes?

It couldn't have been Pete's. He has gray eyes. *I* have brown eyes, but then a lot of other people do, too. And, of course, Jill and Sunny had also said something about a raccoon they'd seen along the shore, and raccoons probably have brown eyes.

Yeah, that was probably it, I decided.

She was probably talking about the raccoon.

15

A shooting star burned across the night sky, all the way from the constellation Perseus to the constellation Pegasus.

"Twelve!" said Cornelius. He looked at the luminous digits on his watch. "That's twelve in ten minutes!"

It was late that night, and Cornelius, Pete, and I were up on Cornelius's moon-viewing platform, watching the Perseid meteor shower. The platform was a perfect place for stargazing. It was high in the tree, but sturdily built, with wood braces underneath. You climbed up through a trapdoor onto a simple round platform about six feet across with a low railing around it. Cornelius had built it facing out toward the lake so you had a really open view of the sky.

"There's another one!" said Pete.

"Thirteen," said Cornelius.

Cornelius hadn't known anything about meteor showers or shooting stars. He'd said he'd noticed there were a lot of shooting stars the last couple of nights, but he hadn't known why. He'd said he didn't even really know what a shooting star was. Of course, I didn't know all that much myself, but I'd told him what I knew.

I told him that the scientific name for a shooting star is "meteor," and that it's the streak of light caused by a small particle—usually no larger than a grain of sand—striking the earth's atmosphere and burning up. Several times a year the earth passes through swarms of particles, which are usually the remains of a comet, and then you get meteor showers. Most people think the Perseid meteor shower is the best one of the year. It has its peak on August 11, and the best time to watch it is after midnight, when you can see about one meteor a minute.

For a long time we watched the meteor shower, sitting cross-legged on the platform, facing north over the lake toward the constellation Perseus.

84

We were higher than I'd ever been in a tree before, and it almost felt like we were on a magic carpet.

As we watched, we talked about astronomy. Cornelius must have asked me a hundred questions about everything from cosmic rays to quasars. I'm no expert, of course, but since astronomy is sort of a hobby of mine, I was able to answer a lot of them.

Cornelius was interested in everything, but what really got him was when I pointed out the great galaxy in Andromeda.

"Two hundred billion stars?" he said. "That little fuzzy thing has two hundred billion stars in it?"

It *is* pretty hard to believe. I mean, it's just this hazy little blotch of light that hardly looks any bigger than a star—and is much fainter than most stars. In fact, a lot of people can't even see it without binoculars or a telescope.

But that tiny fuzzy spot is actually an entire galaxy of stars. It only looks small because it's so far away—two million light-years away. Farther away than anything else you can see with the naked eye.

"It's a spiral galaxy," I added, "just like ours."

Cornelius borrowed my binoculars and took a closer look. "It does look sort of oval-shaped," he said, sounding amazed. He studied it for a while and then passed the binoculars to Pete. *"Two hundred billion stars!"* he repeated.

Cornelius was overcome.

"Just think!" he burst out, his voice full of wonder. "Just think of all the planets that must be revolving around all the stars within that tiny speck of light. All the worlds we'll never know! All the extraordinary life forms we'll never see! All the fantastic thoughts being thought! All the strange and alien civilizations!" He paused and then added emotionally, "I don't mind telling you, it fills me with awe and humility."

Cornelius fell silent, gazing up toward Andromeda. I was pretty overcome myself. There is nothing, I thought as another shooting star streaked across the sky, so uplifting as contemplating the night sky. So awe-inspiring. So—

Suddenly Pete broke the silence.

"Say, did either of you guys ever see *The Slime from Outer Space*?" he wanted to know. "It was this real neat movie about this purple gunky stuff from outer space that tries to take over the world. Boy! Yuck! It was great!"

I rolled my eyes. How could Pete bring up some old movie about a bunch of purple gunk at a time like this? I mean, here we were, on a *moon-viewing platform*. A place for quiet contemplation. A place to reflect upon the larger questions of

86

life. Upon mankind's role in the universe, for instance. Upon the mystery of life itself, for instance.

It was embarrassing. *Purple gunk?* I mean, what was Cornelius going to think? He was probably going to order us right off his platform.

Cornelius cleared his throat.

"You bet!" he said eagerly. "I've seen it six times. Wow, what a movie! Remember when the Purple Slime came oozing up out of the sewer system and started up the Empire State Building, floor by floor? Yugh! Was that *repulsive?* Remember that slimy slurping sound it made when it glopped all over the coffee machines and started eating them? I thought I was going to be sick. Wow! When was the last time you saw it?"

I couldn't believe it. Cornelius, too?

"About a month ago, on the late movie," said Pete. "It's one of the best movies I've ever seen. Remember when the Air Force came, and the Purple Slime was trying to decide what to do? And its huge brain was just sort of sitting there quivering like some kind of purplish-black jelly, only more disgusting?"

"Yeah," said Cornelius, "and then remember how it decided to retreat, so it dribbled out all the windows and down the sides of the whole building and back into the sewer?"

"And that's when it ate all those rats! Remember that big pile of rat skeletons?"

"Yeah, gross!" said Cornelius. "But Pete, I think that came before, didn't it? I think the Slime ate the rats *before* it attacked the Empire State Building."

"No," said Pete, shaking his head, "I think it was after, wasn't it?"

"I don't know. It seems to me it was before."

"I'm pretty sure it was after."

"No, I really think it was before."

"I still think it was after."

The time had come for me to speak. After all, enough was enough. I couldn't help it. I just had to say something.

"I'm almost positive," I told them, "that it was *before*."

"Oh?" said Pete and Cornelius together.

"Yeah," I said. "See, the Purple Slime ate the rats right after it ate the police car and just before it tried to eat Professor Hendricks and his girlfriend Trixie. Remember? It was just finishing off the rats when it saw the Professor and Trixie, and then it chased them and they escaped up through the manhole, and that's when the Purple Slime came up after them and saw the Empire State Building."

"That's right!" said Pete. "Sure. Now I remember. It sort of lunged at Trixie as she was climbing out of the sewer and almost got her."

"Yeah, ugh," I said, shuddering. "It got her shoe and sucked it right off her foot."

"What'd you think about the beginning?" Cornelius asked us. "Wasn't that great? When Trixie was in her kitchen, all alone, and the Purple Slime came bubbling up out of the sink, and she had her back turned, and it started oozing toward her across the kitchen counter, and it . . ."

16

Pete had a funny feeling.

"I've got this funny feeling," said Pete.

It was the next morning and we were sitting on top of Mount Mysterious, which is what Pete had decided to call the big hill that was the high point on the island. Pete had just finished making our official Turtle Island flag. Using some marker pens and a big rectangle that he'd cut out of an old T-shirt, he'd drawn a picture of two smiling turtles facing each other—Snowball and Poopsie, of course. Then he'd attached the flag to a long stick and mounted the stick vertically, wedging it between two big rocks.

Meanwhile, I'd been working on our official Turtle Island map, using a piece of parchment-type paper and a box of colored pencils. I'd carefully drawn the outline of the island in black and then used different colors for the various features: Hidden Valley, Bullfrog Lagoon, Cove of the Screaming Ghost, Cornelius's Tree House, Mount Mysterious, and, of course, the Enemy Camp.

The map looked good. I rolled it up.

"What sort of funny feeling?" I asked him.

"I don't know. It's weird. I have this funny feeling that the girls are going to find our tent. Our Tiny Tot Tent."

I don't believe in funny feelings. I believe in facts.

"Don't be ridiculous," I scoffed. "Forget it. Nobody could find our tent."

Still, I thought to myself, maybe I was being too hasty. I mean, when you happen to be living in a Hänsel and Gretel's Gingerbread House Tent, with a plastic cobblestone sidewalk and little windows with frilly curtains, you can't afford to take chances. You have to be more careful than other people. You have to keep an open mind about everything, including funny feelings.

"Pete," I said, "tell me more about this funny feeling."

He shrugged. "I don't know," he said with a puzzled frown. "It's kind of hard to describe. I've had it ever since we got up this morning, and it's been getting stronger and stronger. It's just this real weird feeling that the girls are out looking for our camp and that they're going to find it—and our tent, too. And laugh themselves silly when they do."

"Hmmmm," I said.

I was beginning to feel a little uneasy myself.

What if they *did* find it? A vision of our tent passed in front of my eyes. All those candy canes! All those gumdrops! And there was Jill, standing in front of it, pointing at it, looking as if she couldn't believe her eyes. Now she was cracking up, both hands clapped over her mouth. Now she was collapsing to her knees, tears rolling down her cheeks. . . .

I shuddered.

It certainly made sense that the girls would be looking for us. After all, how else were they going to get even with us for yesterday? They weren't quitters, that was for sure. They'd *have* to come looking for us. It's exactly what Pete and I would do if we were in their shoes.

I could see it now. They'd figure we'd have to

be camping near water. And since there weren't any streams on the island, that meant we'd be near the shore. So how long could it take them to find us? One day? Two? I mean, Turtle Island was big, but it wasn't *that* big.

A funny feeling with icy little feet galloped up my spine. I could feel myself beginning to panic.

"Uh, say, Pete," I said, trying to sound calm and casual. "You know what? I have sort of an idea."

"Yeah?" he said.

"Yeah, listen. How about if we go on back to camp and take down our tent? You know, just to be on the safe side. We could take it down and stuff it in its bag and hide it somewhere. What do you think?"

"The sooner the better," said Pete without hesitation.

I stood up.

"Pete," I said.

Pete stood up.

"Let's run," I said.

"Right!" he said.

We went tearing down the hill at breakneck speed.

Inside our tent I scrambled across the floor, grabbing up a sock, a book, a flashlight. I tossed them to Pete, and he jammed them into a duffel bag. I looked quickly around the tent, spotted my jacket in a corner, and dived for it.

This was ridiculous. I knew it was ridiculous. Why were we so worried? The girls were probably miles away.

This is what happens, I told myself, when you let funny feelings get ahold of you. You start thinking crazy things. Things like: **THEY COULD BE HERE ANY MINUTE**!

I grabbed my jacket and threw it to Pete. He crammed it, jammed it, stuffed it.

Now for our sleeping bags. We scrambled over and started rolling them up—

"Sunny!" called a girl's voice from somewhere outside. "Sunny! Come here, quick. There's some kind of tent over here!"

Pete and I froze, kneeling over our partly rolled-up bags. I'd know that voice anywhere. It was Jill's.

"I'll be right there," Sunny called back. She sounded farther away, like she was just squeezing past the big rock.

"Come on," called Jill excitedly. "It's adorable! It's got a chimney and candy canes and gumdrops and everything! It's *darling*!"

Pete and I stared at each other in panic. Pete's eyes were bugging out. I think mine were, too.

"Oh, it's precious!" exclaimed Sunny, arriving.

"It's right out of a fairy tale. But whose is it?"

"It must belong to some little bitty kids," said Jill. "Hello-o-o!" she called. "Anybody home?"

Pete and I didn't even breathe.

"Yeah, but what about their mommy and daddy?" asked Sunny. "Where's their tent?"

"I don't know. Somewhere on the other side of the rock, maybe. Maybe they let the kiddies stay over here so they'd feel like big people."

"Isn't it *cute*?" gushed Sunny. "See the little sign over the door? 'Hänsel and Gretel's Gingerbread House.' And look at the frosting on the roof! Doesn't it look yummy?"

"You know who'd just *love* this tent?" said Jill. "My little brother, Scooter. He's four years old."

All the color had drained out of Pete's face.

"Let's peek inside," said Jill.

Pete grabbed my arm with both hands. His expression said: *Don't just stand there! Do something!*

I looked around wildly for someplace to hide. There wasn't any place! Sure, we could get into our sleeping bags, but what good would that do? I could just see it. They'd come in, and there we'd be, lying side by side, with just our heads sticking out, grinning foolishly—all tucked in for our morning nap.

"We can't go in there," objected Sunny. "It doesn't belong to us."

"I know, but we won't go all the way in. We'll just peek. Don't you want to see what it's like inside?"

We had to get out of there! They were coming in. I *knew* they were coming in. I motioned to Pete and, taking giant tiptoe steps, we sneaked over to the window at the back of the tent. My heart was pounding as I began quickly unzipping the flap.

"I don't think we should," said Sunny primly. "What if somebody came back?"

That's right! I wanted to yell. *What if somebody came back?*

"So?" reasoned Jill. "What if they did? It'd just be some little kids. We'd tell them we just wanted to see inside their Gingerbread House. Maybe we'd tell them a bedtime story or something. Come on. I bet it's as cute as a button inside."

The zipper was stuck! The lousy, rotten zipper was stuck! I almost had it unzipped and then it stuck. I started shaking it desperately, tugging at it. Pete was practically climbing over my back, reaching around me, his hands on top of mine, shaking, tugging. I couldn't see what I was doing. *"Pete!"* I hissed under my breath. *"Will you let go of me?"*

"Well, all right," said Sunny reluctantly. "But just a peek. Okay?"

No!

"Okay," said Jill.

The zipper came loose! I quickly eased it down the rest of the way.

"These cobblestones look so *real*," exclaimed Sunny. Her voice was really close now, right outside the door. "And look here. Look at the doorknob. It's a cookie!"

I threw open the window flap and started through.

So did Pete. At the *same time*. We got stuck!

Wedged in and tangled up, we struggled to get free. Wriggling, twisting. It was every man for himself. I had my hand on top of Pete's head and was pushing down, trying to pry myself past him. Pete had his elbow in my cheek.

"Hi, guys!"

We looked up.

There, outside, were Jill and Sunny. Peering around the left side of the tent, grinning from ear to ear.

"Here. Just let us get your picture," said Jill brightly.

She skipped out in front of us.

"Say cheese!" said Sunny.

Jill aimed her camera at us, and I heard that old familiar click.

"By the way," said Jill sweetly as she buttoned

her camera case closed. "Which one of you is Hänsel, and which one is Gretel?"

"**GIMME THAT CAMERA**!" roared Pete, lunging at them. The whole tent wobbled and tilted and almost collapsed before Pete broke free and went tumbling out the window in a heap.

The girls took off like a shot, laughing like loons. They dived through the trees, scrambled down to the water, and—just as Pete and I were getting up some speed—pushed off in their canoe.

Pete and I charged over toward our canoe.

Where *was* it? It was gone!

"Oh, by the way," called Sunny. "We had a little free time while we were waiting for you, so we hid your canoe."

Free time? Waiting for us?

So they'd been here all along!

Jill waggled her fingers good-bye.

"Toodle-oo!" she called.

17

It's always darkest before the dawn, they say. Which is supposed to mean that when things look really bad, you can usually expect a change for the better.

It didn't work. Things got worse.

Pete and I found our canoe, which the girls had hidden in some trees nearby, and brought it back to camp. Then we spent a little while kicking things—trees mostly. And finally we plodded on over to Cornelius's. We'd promised to help him fix something on his tree house, something he called his Super Duper. Right away when we got there, he gleefully told us the news—the girls were coming to tea.

Pete and I stared at him.

Cornelius went on. He said he'd run into Jill's Aunt Katherine again earlier that morning when he was out in his rowboat fishing. She'd come paddling by in her canoe and he'd found the courage to invite her over for afternoon tea. He'd asked her to bring along those two charming girls, Jill and Sunny, and he'd assured her that Pete and I would be there, too. He'd told her we wouldn't want to miss it for the world.

My mind reeled, and for a few seconds Pete and I were too stunned to speak. Finally, Pete managed to blurt out, "Sorry. Can't make it. We're going to Mongolia."

Cornelius looked confused. So I apologized to him and told him that it was very nice of him to invite us, but that our relationship with Jill and Sunny was a little rocky at the moment, so it wouldn't be possible for us to have tea with them. We'd rather die a thousand deaths first.

Now Cornelius *really* looked confused. He said he respected our feelings, but he couldn't help wondering what in the world could have happened to make us feel so strongly about Jill and Sunny.

We did sort of owe him an explanation. So we

started to tell him just one or two little things— about how we'd capsized our canoe the day we arrived and how the girls had had the time of their lives taking our pictures. But what with Pete and me interrupting each other and adding on more and more details, and what with Cornelius asking questions and looking so interested, it wasn't long before we'd spilled the whole story. All about Mr. Moose and Mr. Duck, and the Wolverine Attack, and Snowball and Poopsie, and the Gingerbread Tent, and everything.

"Mmmmm," said Cornelius after we'd finished. "I see what you mean. That's a pretty rocky relationship, all right."

"The worst," said Pete. "The pits."

"Exactly," said Cornelius crisply. "And that's why this tea party is just what the doctor ordered."

Pete and I looked at each other and then back at Cornelius.

"No, really, Cornelius," I began, "I don't think you understand. You see—"

"Trust me," he said, holding up his hand. "Believe me, you'll thank me later. This party is going to give you boys a chance to get off on an entirely new foot with Jill and Sunny."

Pete snorted. "When it comes to Jill and Sunny," he muttered, "there's only one thing I'd like to do with my foot."

Cornelius didn't hear him. He'd started pacing back and forth, with a sort of dreamy, enthusiastic look on his face. We were up on his breakfast balcony, which was about twenty feet long, so he had plenty of room to pace. I had the sinking feeling he was about to go philosophical on us. And he did.

"Boys," he said grandly. "This isn't just a chance for me to get to know Katherine better and maybe impress her with my jungle skills; this is a chance for us to bring peace and harmony to this splendid island of ours."

Jungle skills?

"What a wonderful opportunity we have! To forgive and forget. To live and let live. To let bygones be bygones, and to build bridges of human understanding. All we have to do is open up our hearts and let the sun shine in!"

"No way," said Pete and I together.

"Besides," Cornelius added, sort of as an afterthought, "I already told Katherine you were coming over. What will Jill and Sunny think if you leave before they get here?"

Uh-oh. Good point.

They'd think we were chicken, that's what. Too scared to face them. I winced. Great. That'd be just great. Moose and Duck Chicken, at your service.

"Yeah, well, uh, what do you think, Pete?" I asked. "I mean, if we don't show up, the girls might think we were, uh . . . you know . . . not too brave. I mean, we wouldn't want them to . . . uh . . . die laughing."

Pete sighed. "Yeah, I see what you mean," he said glumly. "I guess we've got no choice. I mean, I guess a guy's gotta do what a guy's gotta do. So I guess we gotta go to a tea party."

"You won't regret it!" said Cornelius cheerfully.

Pete slouched against the railing of the balcony, staring gloomily down at the inlet. Suddenly, something occurred to him, and he perked up slightly.

"Say, Cornelius," he said, "if they give us any trouble, can we throw them in the lake?"

"Now don't you worry," said Cornelius. "You won't have to. Mark my words, those two young ladies are going to charm your socks off."

So it was settled. If I'd had my social calendar with me, I'd have made an entry in it: "Tea at three."

"Are you sure this is strong enough?" I asked, eyeing the thin nylon rope stretching away through the forest.

We were standing on a small platform near

Cornelius's library, up in the first tree. Jill, Sunny, and Aunt Katherine weren't coming till the middle of the afternoon, so we'd had plenty of time to help Cornelius with his new project—his Super Duper.

"You bet," said Cornelius. "That rope is five-thousand-pound test."

The Super Duper had turned out to be a "secret high-speed escape route," as Cornelius put it. Every tree house, Cornelius said, should have a secret high-speed escape route. Just in case.

What the Super Duper actually was was a hundred-foot-long rope slide. We'd rigged it up by first tying one end of the rope to the trunk of the tree just behind the platform—about thirty feet above the ground. Then we'd tied the other end to a tree far away through the forest—this time only about four feet above the ground. Working together, we'd managed to get the rope stretched taut before we'd tied it at the lower end. Finally, mounted on the rope was a sailboat block, with its pulley rolling freely along the top of the rope. And under the rope, hanging down from the frame of the block, was a large wooden handle, wide enough to grip with both hands.

Presto! A Super Duper! Of course, we hadn't tested it yet, but if everything went as planned, we would have a long, fast, sloping ride from the platform down through the forest—over the branches of one tree, under the branches of another—all the way to a soft landing on a small grassy patch of ground deep in the woods.

Cornelius had figured out a neat way to get the pulley back up, too. He had an extra fishing reel that we attached to the tree near the top of the rope. Then we hooked the fishing line to the pulley. When someone went zooming down the rope, the fishing line would unreel after him. All you'd have to do then was reel the pulley back up the rope.

Cornelius looked really happy with his new Super Duper.

"Every tree house," he declared again as we surveyed our work from the launching platform, "should have at least one of these." He was standing on the edge of the platform, ready for his first test run. He had both hands above him, grasping the handle of the sailboat block, sliding it back and forth along the rope. His knees were bent. His eyes were narrowed. "A tree house without a secret high-speed escape route is nothing less than an invitation to trouble.

"Suppose, for instance," he went on dramatically, "that your tree house is suddenly invaded by a whole batallion of army ants, or maybe by a gang of ruthless criminals."

Sometimes, I told myself, Cornelius reminded me of Pete. I didn't know why exactly. He just did.

"Yeah!" said Pete eagerly. "Or maybe by a band of bloodthirsty baboons, led by their leader baboon, Kong."

"Right!" said Cornelius. "Maybe fifty of them. And they come after me, see, howling and baring their fangs."

"They're everywhere," said Pete. "Swarming after you, frothing at the mouth. You put up a brave fight, but there are too many of them!"

"They've almost got me cornered," said Cornelius. "But then suddenly I remember my Super Duper!"

"Your secret high-speed escape route!" said Pete.

"I fight my way here to the platform, karate chopping right and left," said Cornelius. "I grab ahold of the Super Duper!"

"They're almost here!" said Pete. "There's not much time!"

Suddenly, Cornelius took a giant leap and launched himself off the platform. He went whizzing away down the rope.

"**THEY'LL NEVER TAKE ME ALIVE!**" he yelled back over his shoulder.

Yes, I thought to myself, there definitely are times when Cornelius reminds me of Pete.

18

Our guests arrived right on time.

I spotted them through my binoculars from my lookout up in the crow's nest, which was the bottom half of a wooden barrel mounted in the fork of two branches high in the middle tree. There they were—Jill, Sunny, and Jill's Aunt Katherine—about two hundred yards away, crossing an open area where the trail went over a low rise.

Aunt Katherine was in the lead, tramping along wearing sturdy hiking boots, rugged khaki shorts with lots of pockets, a camera over her shoulder, and a green T-shirt that said "Mount Kilimanjaro" on it. I could sort of see why Cornelius liked her. She looked as though she *belonged* out on the trail. Of course, Cornelius had put it even stronger. He'd said, "She'd be at home in any desert or jungle on earth." And naturally, he'd followed that up with, "What a woman!"

Jill and Sunny were close behind, in T-shirts and jeans, chatting away. Jill was putting a lot of energy into whatever it was she was saying, waving her arms around and tossing her ponytail. I hoped she was only describing how to do aerobic exercises for the arms and neck, or something like that. But from the way Sunny was laughing, I had the feeling she was describing Pete and me trying to escape from the Gingerbread Tent. I gritted my teeth.

Pete was on a branch about ten feet below me. "They're coming," I reported. "And they're laughing."

Pete groaned.

We climbed down to the breakfast balcony and told Cornelius they were almost here. His face lit up and I thought he was going to kick up his heels or do a jig or something. He combed his hair and tucked in his shirttail. Then he charged over to the edge of the balcony and peered over, trying to catch a glimpse of them as they came out at the head of the inlet.

Soon they appeared, looking like a miniature expedition because they all three had day packs on their backs. Looking up, they caught sight of the tree house for the first time and stopped dead in their tracks. They stared in amazement.

I couldn't blame them. It was a pretty great tree house.

A few minutes later, we were all up on the balcony together, and everyone was introducing each other to everyone. If Jill's aunt recognized Pete and me, she didn't say so. She just gave us each a firm, friendly handshake and told us to call her Katherine.

Sunny stuck out her hand for Pete to shake and said, very politely, "How do you do?"

Pete shook her hand. It was against his principles, but what could he do?

Jill stuck out her hand for me to shake and said, very politely, "How do you *canoe*?" She grinned, and Sunny broke into giggles.

Very funny. I made a grab at her hand, having a couple of good ideas for what I might do with it, but she snatched it back before I could get it.

Katherine shot Jill and Sunny a warning look

that seemed to say, "Now, girls, don't forget we're guests here." Jill and Sunny put on sweet, innocent, wide-eyed looks.

Cornelius's tree house was a big hit. They all loved it. Katherine, especially, was really impressed. "It's wonderful!" she said.

She looked around admiringly. The breakfast balcony was long and narrow, with a hammock at one end of it, strung up between two branches. At the other end was a rustic wooden table and chairs, and over the table, hanging from a branch, was an old brass lantern. The whole balcony was shady and cool.

Behind the balcony was the living room, which was Cornelius's weirdest room, because it was built around the tree so that the tree trunk came right up through the middle of the room. Through the open door and windows, you could see some of the inside walls, which Cornelius had covered from floor to ceiling with his collection of maps.

And when you looked out at the trees on either side of the balcony, you saw suspension bridges and platforms and rooms scattered all around.

"What a fun place to live!" said Katherine.

"Cornelius built it all by himself," volunteered Pete.

"Really?" she said, looking at Cornelius with respect. "You're very talented."

111

Cornelius beamed and blushed at the same time.

One thing was for sure. Things were going a lot better for Cornelius than they had the first time he'd met Katherine, when he'd squashed her camera case and broken her fake tree.

Katherine and the girls asked if they could have a tour of the tree house, so Cornelius said, "We'd be happy to show you around, wouldn't we, boys?" and off we went, with Cornelius and Katherine in the lead.

Jill and I were last. We almost bumped into each other starting across the first suspension bridge.

"After you," she said, standing aside and indicating the bridge with a sweep of her hand.

"No, after you," I said, bowing deeply.

"No, really, I wouldn't hear of it," she said. "It wouldn't be polite. Please, after you."

"No, I beg you," I said, with my hand over my heart. "I couldn't live with myself. Really. Truly. After you."

"No, I couldn't possibly," she said. "I'd hate myself. Believe me. I'd—"

"Aren't you two coming?" called Katherine from high in the next tree.

Jill dived onto the bridge and galloped across. "Last one over is a rotten egg!" she called over her shoulder.

I must be crazy, I thought as I followed her across the bridge. Why do I find myself actually *liking* this girl?

We caught up with everybody in the workshop, where Katherine was admiring one of Cornelius's projects: a cutting board he was making for his kitchen. It was in the shape of an elephant.

"It's charming!" said Katherine, holding it up in front of her. She looked at Cornelius. "I can tell you're an animal lover."

"I *am*," Cornelius assured her. "I *am* an animal lover. And I especially love elephants. In fact, I've always wished I could have an elephant for a pet."

"Well, I think you'd make a wonderful elephant owner," said Katherine firmly. "You're just the sort of person an elephant would trust."

"I hope so," said Cornelius, blushing. "I hope so."

That's sort of the way the tour went. Katherine seemed to be having a great time, and Cornelius, of course, was floating around on a cloud. They talked about everything. She asked him all kinds of questions about his tree house, and he asked her all kinds of questions about cameras and safaris and how to sneak up on birds.

Then we got to Cornelius's writing room. Katherine hadn't known he was a mystery writer, and now she was *really* impressed.

"I'd love to read this, Cornelius!" she said after reading the review on the back of one of his Max Malone books. It was called *Skull and Crossfire*.

"Take it, it's yours!" burst out Cornelius. And for a second there I thought he was going to add, "Everything I *have* is yours!" but he didn't.

If things went on like this, I figured Cornelius and Katherine would get engaged before the afternoon was over.

But things *didn't* go on like that.

Not by a long shot.

19

It all started after we got back down to the living room and were looking at Cornelius's collection of maps.

He had all kinds of them, all over the walls. One of them, for instance, had big sweeping arrows that showed the flyways used by migrating birds. Another had little pictures on it showing the location of Mayan ruins in Mexico and Guatemala. Another was an old, yellowed map of the world that had countries on it that didn't even exist anymore. He must have had fifty maps at least, all of them different.

Jill and Sunny were wandering around together and happened to stop in front of one showing the Galápagos Islands. Up in the corner of the map was a picture of two giant tortoises, crawling along the ground.

Pete and I came up from behind and peered over the girls' shoulders.

"Pete!" I cried, pointing at the tortoises. "Those pictures! Look who it is! Can it be?"

"Holy cow, Scott! You're right! It's . . . it's . . ."

"Snowball and Poopsie!" we said together.

We guffawed and got each other in the side with our elbows while Jill and Sunny glared at us. I noticed that Jill's ears got a little pink.

"Oh, yeah?" said Sunny. "Well, for your information—"

"You should have *seen* yourselves!" said Pete, warming to his topic. "Trying to shake hands with a turtle! Boy, did you look—"

An adult voice rang out from behind us.

"Now, boys," scolded Cornelius.

"Now, girls," said Katherine.

Oops. Caught in the act.

"Let's remember that this is a small island . . ." Cornelius went on.

". . . and that we've all got to live together . . ." added Katherine.

". . . in peace and harmony . . ." said Cornelius.

116

". . . like one big happy family," concluded Katherine.

Cornelius and Katherine exchanged a delighted look, and then Cornelius turned to Pete and me, smiling with kindly understanding.

"Boys," he said solemnly, "I know you have a sort of competition going with Jill and Sunny here. A sort of contest of wits. Now, I'm certainly not saying that competition is always bad. Competition is often a good and healthy thing. But *only*, I think you would agree, if the sides are evenly matched. And therefore," he concluded sweepingly, "I suggest a truce. After all, we wouldn't want these two fine girls to get in over their heads."

Katherine, who had been leaning forward, ready to agree with Cornelius, suddenly stopped with her mouth still open. Slowly she turned to Cornelius, her eyebrows raised.

"Excuse me, Cornelius," she said politely.

"Yes, Katherine?"

"May I inquire exactly what you mean by '*over their heads*'?"

"Oh, why, uh, nothing," said Cornelius, sounding flustered. "Jill and Sunny are two very, very clever girls—anyone can see that. It's just that I happen to know these boys quite well, and they make a very formidable team. I mean, I'm afraid that in this case the girls may have bitten off a bit more than they can chew."

Katherine's eyes narrowed, and they took on a flinty, determined look. The same look, I thought to myself, that had probably made whole herds of lions say to each other, "Head for the hills, men! It's Aunt Katherine!"

Cornelius began to sense that something was wrong. He coughed nervously.

Finally Katherine spoke.

"Ha!" she said.

"Ha?"

"You heard me. Ha!"

Cornelius drew himself up with dignity. "I see," he said stiffly.

"Let me assure you," snapped Katherine, "that Jill and Sunny are perfectly capable of taking care of themselves. Especially on an island such as this one. After all, I've taught them almost everything I know about living in the wilderness."

Cornelius wasn't going to take that lying down. "Is that so?" he said huffily. "Well, it may interest you to know that I've taught Scott and Pete a few things myself. About jungle skills, mostly. This very morning we were studying the concept of a high-speed escape route from your typical jungle dwelling. I think I can safely say these boys are ready for anything."

"Is that so?" said Katherine. "Well, it may interest *you* to know that Jill and Sunny are very nearly *experts* in the flora and fauna of the island habitat. And, I might add, they are second to none when it comes to the care and handling of a canoe."

Jill and Sunny looked surprised at this news. I had the feeling Katherine might be exaggerating a little.

"Is that a fact?" said Cornelius. "Well, it may interest *you* to know that Scott, here, is nothing less than a *genius* when it comes to navigating by the stars. There's not a star in the sky that he doesn't know. And Pete," he went on, "is a natural-born tracker. He can track anything, human or otherwise. You'll notice he wears a buckskin shirt and has a hunting horn."

Katherine snorted. "Are you finished?" she asked.

"Oh, I think so," said Cornelius, enjoying himself. He draped his arms around Pete's and my shoulders. "What more can I say? I think it's obvious that Scott and Pete and I make a pret-ty good team!"

Katherine gave Cornelius a long, cool look,

nodding her head slowly, sizing him up.

Finally she spoke. "In that case, Cornelius, how would you like to pit *your* pret-ty good team against *our* pret-ty good team?"

"Huh?" croaked Cornelius.

Katherine moved over and draped her arms around Jill and Sunny's shoulders. "A little contest, you might say. A little test of skill and wits." She paused. "Unless, of course, you're afraid you'd be biting off more than you can chew."

That did it. Cornelius threw back his shoulders and thrust out his jaw. I think he was trying to suck in his stomach, too.

"You're on!" he said.

20

In no time flat, we'd all agreed on the terms of the Great Turtle Island Flag Race.

"So that's it," said Katherine, summing up. "The first team to get to the top of the big hill—"

"Mount Mysterious," Pete put in.

"—Mount Mysterious, and get the flag that the boys put up there this morning—"

"The one with a picture of two turtles on it," said Pete.

"Snowball and Poopsie," I added helpfully.

"—with Snowball and Poopsie on it," Kather-

121

ine went on, "and bring it back up here to this living room—"

"—are the winners and undisputed All-Time Champions of Turtle Island!" finished Cornelius.

"Agreed," said Katherine crisply.

"And the *losing* team," said Jill, looking at me with a sparkle in her blue eyes, "has to cook three meals a day for two whole days for the winning team."

"And wash all the dishes, too," added Sunny.

"Agreed," said Cornelius.

"I like my eggs scrambled," I told Jill.

"And *please*," said Pete. "No runny eggs. Runny eggs disgust me."

Jill and Sunny began jogging in place. "Did you know," Jill asked me sweetly, "that Sunny is on the track team at our school? Her coach says he hasn't seen a girl with such long legs and such a smooth stride in years. He says she runs like a gazelle."

I watched Sunny jog in place for a few seconds, and then I gave a sort of snort as if to say, "Ha! You think we're scared of *her*?" Then I swallowed hard. Oh, no, I thought to myself, she looks like she can outrun a car.

"Let's see now," said Cornelius. "What about the rules? I mean, shouldn't we decide what's fair and what's not f—"

"Rules, shmules," interrupted Katherine, with

a wave of her hand. "Who needs rules? It's simple enough. Whichever team gets back up here to this room with the flag is the winner. Until then, anything goes. Shortcuts, ambushes, anything."

"*Ambushes?*" said Cornelius.

"What about tackling?" said Pete.

"Sure," said Katherine. "If you think you can catch us. Now if you'll excuse me for a few minutes, I think I'll limber up a bit." She put her feet wide apart, legs straight, and began energetically touching first her right toes, then her left. Right, left, right, left.

"Aunt Katherine jogs six miles a day," Jill informed us.

Suddenly, I had this vision of Katherine jogging up the side of Mount Kilimanjaro. She had a huge backpack on her back, with a rolled-up tent, a sleeping bag, and a couple of cast-iron frying pans tied to it. She wasn't even breathing hard.

"Boys," said Cornelius nonchalantly, "I'm sure you'll agree we have no need to limber up. So why don't we just step outside for a few minutes to plan our strategy?"

"Right," said Pete and I together. We started out the door after Cornelius.

"Take your time," Jill called after us. "You guys are going to need all the strategy you can get."

Yeah, I thought to myself. And our own personal hundred-mile-an-hour tail wind wouldn't hurt, either.

"Uh, Cornelius," I said, "I'm not sure I heard you right. Could you say that again?"

We'd crossed a suspension bridge to the third tree—for privacy—and were in a sort of huddle, out on the rope-swinging platform, speaking in lowered voices.

"Surely," said Cornelius. "I said that we might consider putting all the rope ladders out of commission."

I blinked. "I still don't—"

"You see," explained Cornelius, "all we'd have to do is pull up each of the three rope ladders—the ones that go from each tree down to the ground—and tie them in knots. Then when the race begins, we could make our getaway using the rope swing and the Super Duper. Katherine and the girls would be stuck in the tree house—at least until they managed to untie the rope ladders. Which should take them three or four minutes, I should think."

He looked back and forth between Pete and me with satisfaction. "Well, that's it in a nutshell," he said. "The three of us would be off for Mount

124

Mysterious with a healthy head start under our belts and victory in the bag. What do you think?"

"Terrific!" said Pete. "Let's go for it!"

"But Cornelius," I said, "are you sure it's . . . well . . . fair for us to tie up the ladders?"

"I understand your concern," said Cornelius, glancing back over his shoulder. "Naturally, we wouldn't want to do anything that isn't absolutely fair and square. But fortunately Katherine did specifically say, 'Rules, shmules,' and I think we are entitled to use that as our guideline, don't you agree?"

Good point.

"Okay, let's go for it," I said.

"All right," said Cornelius. "Now—"

"Except for one thing," I said. "How can we use the rope swing? None of us has ever been able to make it all the way across the inlet to the other platform."

"Don't worry," said Cornelius, brimming with confidence. "I'll be the one to use the rope swing, and this time I *know* I can make it. I'll just give my Tarzan yell and think about how good it's going to feel to be the All-Time Champions of Turtle Island. Believe me, it'll be as easy as pie."

"You can do it!" said Pete.

"Thank you," said Cornelius modestly.

125

"Let's see, then," I said. "Pete and I'll go down the Super Duper together, right? In one trip. There won't be time for two trips."

"Right," said Cornelius. "The rope's plenty strong enough. And the handle's wide enough for both of you to hold on to, too."

"We'll leave 'em in our dust," said Pete.

"Now," said Cornelius, "we'd better move fast and get those ladders tied up. I figure we have about four minutes before Katherine and the girls get suspicious."

We split up and went for the rope ladders. Pete took the one just below us, in the third tree; Cornelius sneaked over to the one in the middle tree; and I quickly crossed through the middle tree to the first tree.

The ladder hung down through a trapdoor in a platform about fifteen feet off the ground. Working fast, I pulled the ladder up, made a loop in it, fed the bottom end of the ladder through the loop, and pulled it as tight as I could get it. Then I made another loop, fed the ladder through it, and pulled it tight again. I did that five times, until I'd used up all the ladder.

That should slow them down all right, I thought.

Quickly I sneaked back across the bridge to the middle tree and joined Cornelius outside the living room. A moment later, Pete arrived. The three of us grinned at each other and gave the thumbs-up sign.

Then we went inside.

Katherine and the girls were sitting on the floor with their legs out straight in front of them, holding their ankles and pressing their foreheads against their knees.

"Well, ladies," said Cornelius, "are you ready for the big event?"

They jumped to their feet. "Whenever you are," said Katherine, looking confident.

Jill eyed us. "You guys sure took long enough," she said.

"Yeah," said Sunny. "You must've come up with a real whopper of a plan."

"Afraid not," said Cornelius, shaking his head. He tried to sound discouraged. Then he put his arms around Pete's and my shoulders. "But don't worry, boys," he said dramatically. "We may not have a plan, but we'll give this race our best shot, won't we?"

"We *will*," I said bravely.

"We'll *never* give up," declared Pete.

Cornelius beamed at us proudly. "That's the spirit, boys!" he said. "After all, it's not whether you win or lose, it's how you play the game!"

21

"On your mark!

"Get set!

"**GO**!"

All six of us dive for the living room door.

Katherine is quick and she makes it through first. The rest of us collide in the doorway. Jill tickles me in the ribs and I yelp, leaping into the air. "Ladies first!" she whoops, and squeezes past me out the door. I'm next, followed by Cornelius. Behind us, Sunny and Pete, struggling, are having words. "You're on my foot!" Sunny is squawking. "Gangway!" I hear Pete say.

128

Outside, I glance to the left and see Jill disappearing around the side of the breakfast balcony, heading for the nearest rope ladder. I turn right and sprint along the balcony to the suspension bridge that leads to the first tree. Three quarters of the way across the bridge, I stop and look back.

Here comes Pete, burning rubber. Above him, still in the middle tree, Cornelius has scrambled up a flight of steps and has just reached a bridge leading to the third tree. A few feet below the living room, Katherine and Jill are on a platform, kneeling down, examining a tangled clump of rope. Sunny is just arriving.

"They've tied the ladder in knots!" sputters Katherine.

Now Katherine and Jill are on their feet, looking around fiercely. Jill spots me. Katherine spots Cornelius. They almost knock Sunny over as they charge back up toward the balcony.

"You two go after them!" Katherine shouts. "I'll take Cornelius!"

I spin and race across the bridge. "Let's go!" I yell over my shoulder to Pete.

We bound up the stairs that wind around the trunk and charge out onto the causeway near the library. Somewhere below, we hear the girls scrambling after us. We reach the platform, and

I quickly free the handle of the Super Duper, which is tied loosely to a branch. Pete unhooks the fishing line from the pulley so the girls can't reel it back up after we go down.

Suddenly, a deep, thundering cry splits the air.

It's Cornelius. Giving his Tarzan yell.

Pete and I whirl. I can't see Cornelius because of the leaves, but I do see Katherine. She's over in the third tree, pouring on the steam. She's probably hoping to tackle Cornelius before he can take off. I glance down. Jill and Sunny are just below us on the winding steps. They've stopped, too, and are watching the action in tree number three.

Pete jabs me in the side with his elbow and points through the leaves. There's Cornelius on the rope swing, swooping across the inlet! And there's the platform on the other side. I hold my breath. He's up. His feet are on the platform. He lunges for the hand pole. *He makes it!*

Pete and I cheer wildly. Cornelius raises his arms in triumph and looks over at us, grinning from ear to ear.

"Way to go, Cornelius!" yells Pete.

Cornelius gives us a wave. Then he secures the rope to the hand pole and bounds toward the rope ladder.

We hear a sound. It's the girls! They've sneaked

up the steps and are creeping out the causeway toward us, an evil gleam in their eyes. They're almost on us.

I turn and grab the Super Duper handle with both hands. Beside me, Pete grabs hold too.

"Don't let 'em get away!" yells Jill.

They're too late. We leap off the platform.

And, as free as two birds on the wing, we sail away down through the trees on Cornelius's secret high-speed escape route. The wind in our faces, the girls at our back. We're home free!

"*Whoopeeeeeeee!!!!!*" yells Pete.

We land—a hundred feet away—on the soft green grass, sprawling, laughing. Not a perfect landing, but who cares? We untangle ourselves and jump to our feet.

Pete puts his hunting horn to his lips and gives a long, triumphant blast that knocks a few dry leaves off a nearby tree. I peer back along the rope to the tree house. Sunny is shaking her fist at us. Jill, her hands on her hips, is glaring down at us. They look pretty steamed up.

I waggle my fingers. "Toodle-oo!" I call cheerfully.

Our team—the Turtle Island Trailblazers, as Pete named us—joined up at the head of the inlet and hightailed it up the main trail. About twelve

131

minutes later, with nary a sign of Katherine or the girls, we approached the top of Mount Mysterious. Scrambling up to the top of the pile of boulders, we seized the flagpole and pulled it free of the rocks. We had the flag!

"Nothing to it," said Cornelius, gasping for breath. "Couldn't have been easier."

We all whacked each other on the back, grinning.

Of course, the race wasn't over yet. We still had to get the flag back to the tree house. And the opposing team, we knew, couldn't be far behind us. It couldn't have taken them more than a few minutes to untangle one of the rope ladders.

We slipped down off the boulders, sneaked into the underbrush, and started back by a different route, to avoid an ambush. Moving quickly but quietly, we cut over to the lake on the west side of the island and then made our way north along the shore, stopping now and then to listen for sounds from the girls. We didn't hear a thing. We'd given them the slip.

I chuckled. They were probably lurking somewhere back along the main trail, crouched down behind some bushes, with leering grins on their faces, getting muscle cramps in their legs, waiting to pounce on us and grab the flag. It was nice to know they were going to be disappointed.

As we neared the tree house, I felt my heart beating faster and faster. I couldn't believe it. We were about to become the All-Time Champions of Turtle Island! No more would I be known as Mr. Duck. "From now on," I'd explain to Jill in a kindly voice, "you may call me Mr. Champion. Or, if you prefer, Mr. Champion, *sir*."

We arrived at the inlet.

Pete, who was in such high spirits he was practically bobbing along like a helium balloon, raised his hunting horn to his lips to give a victory blast.

Then we caught sight of the tree house.

We stopped dead in our tracks, and Pete's victory blast came out as a short, flat BLAT!

There were Katherine and the girls, still up in the tree house.

And they didn't look worried, or angry, or defeated. They looked *relaxed*. And *happy*.

Something was up. And it looked like trouble.

Lounging in the hammock that was strung above the breakfast balcony, her head on a pillow and a book in one hand, lay Katherine. She put down the lemonade she'd been sipping and gave us a friendly wave.

133

Jill was there on the balcony, too, tilting back in a chair, her feet up on the railing, using my binoculars to scan the trees on the far side of the inlet. Bird-watching, probably. Behind her, Sunny was lazily juggling three apples.

"Oh, hi!" said Sunny, catching all three apples neatly.

Jill lowered the binoculars and looked at us with mild surprise. "Back so soon?"

I nudged Cornelius. "I don't see any of the rope ladders," I whispered out of the corner of my mouth. "How are we going to get up there?"

"Let's have a closer look," whispered Cornelius. We ambled closer. No rope ladders.

Katherine and the girls had gathered at the edge of the balcony, leaning over, resting their elbows on the railing, grinning down at us.

Cornelius looked up at them. "We won," he said. He didn't sound very convinced. "We have the flag." He waved the flag around a little.

Jill and Sunny giggled.

"Oh, the *flag*," said Katherine brightly. She turned to the girls. "Do you have that basket?" she asked.

"Right here," said Jill. She and Sunny disappeared for a moment and then returned with a big basket with a long rope tied to it.

"Now, if I remember correctly," Katherine went

on pleasantly, "the finish line is not down there where *you* are. It's up here where *we* are. In the living room. So, if you'll just hand the flag over to us, we'll run it in to the finish line."

"Making us the winners and All-Time Champions of Turtle Island," explained Jill.

"And then," finished Sunny, "we'll lower you a rope ladder, and you can have your tree house back."

What? I'd never heard of such a sneaky, underhanded thing in my whole life. Unless, of course, it was our tying up the ladders in the first place.

Suddenly I thought of something. What about using the rope swing to get back into the tree house? Cornelius had made it across the inlet before; maybe he could do it again! Without moving my head, I took a quick, furtive peek over at the rope-swinging platform on the opposite side of the inlet. But the rope wasn't there!

"Sorry, but I'm afraid that the rope swing is not available at the moment," said Jill helpfully. She must have seen me peeking. "You'll notice the rope is on our side of the inlet now. While you were gone, we lowered one of the ladders, and Aunt Katherine went over and threw the rope swing back across to Sunny and me."

She began lowering the basket over the side of

the balcony. "Just put the flag in here," she said.

Cornelius, Pete, and I spoke almost at the same time.

"Fat chance!" said Cornelius.

"Over my dead body!" I said.

"Forget it!" said Pete. "I'd rather wear a rabbit suit for the rest of my life!"

Rabbit suit?

Katherine shrugged. "Very well," she said. "But in that case, you might want to start thinking about where you're going to spend the night. I wouldn't be a bit surprised if it rained."

There was a distant rumble of thunder.

Cornelius, Pete, and I exchanged uncomfortable glances. We had to do *something*. We were going to begin to look pretty stupid just standing there in front of that dangling basket, with Katherine and the girls grinning down at us and a storm coming on.

Cornelius took the bull by the horns. "Boys," he said with dignity, "perhaps we'd best adjourn to your tent while we plan a comprehensive strategy for victory. After all, there's no hurry. We've still got the flag, so we're still sitting pretty. What do you think?"

"Good idea," I said, hoping I sounded as dignified as Cornelius did.

"But we'll be back!" said Pete, glaring up at the girls. "This race isn't over yet."

"It certainly isn't," agreed Cornelius. "Ladies, you haven't seen the last of us!" He tucked the flag under his arm and we started off.

"Oh, by the way, Cornelius," Katherine called after us, "this book of yours is really quite exciting. I'm very impressed. You certainly are a man of many surprises."

She said it like she really meant it.

"Humph," said Cornelius. But I could tell he was kind of pleased.

We stomped off into the forest.

22

"So . . ." said Cornelius for about the fifth time. "So this is your tent."

He kept staring at it, his chin in his hand, nodding his head as he took in all the details. Of course, Pete and I had already told him about our good old Hänsel and Gretel's Gingerbread House Tent, but some things have to be seen to be believed.

"Uh, what's that on the roof?" he asked us. "Is that . . ."

"Frosting," I said.

"Oh."

There was a silence.

"You say the girls actually have a picture of you and this tent?" he asked.

I nodded. "Yeah, we were stuck in the window around on the other side. But don't worry, we're going to get that picture back and destroy it."

"Or die," said Pete.

The storm was approaching. The sky had darkened, and the wind was picking up. It began to sprinkle as Cornelius, Pete, and I ducked inside the tent.

Using sleeping bags and jackets to lean up against, we made ourselves comfortable on the floor and broke out some granola bars and oranges. I noticed Cornelius peeking at the wicked witch, but of course he was too polite to mention it.

"Nice and roomy in here," he said.

We began to discuss Katherine and the girls. We all agreed we needed a plan, and Pete said he had one. He said we should attack at midnight. He said we should creep up on the tree house, throw a rope over one of the limbs, tie a slipknot in the rope, climb up, sneak the flag into the living room, and then wake everybody up, yelling and cheering.

I pointed out that we didn't have a rope.

Pete looked stumped.

So did Cornelius. He agreed that not having a rope was going to make things tricky. He said, however, that we weren't licked yet, and by the way, could we remember the exact words that Katherine had used when she complimented him on his book?

I said yes, I thought I could remember her exact words. I said she'd said, "Oh, by the way, Cornelius, this book of yours is really quite exciting. I'm very impressed. You certainly are a man of many surprises."

Pete said how about if we tied a whole bunch of shirts and jackets and sleeping bags and stuff together to *make* a rope.

I said we might be able to do that, but I still didn't think the plan was going to work. I said I couldn't believe that Jill and Sunny and Katherine wouldn't have someone on watch all night long. I said we'd learned the hard way that they weren't easy to fool. They were smart and tough—we had to give them credit for that.

Cornelius said he agreed that they were very smart, all right, and by the way, was I sure that Katherine had said he was "a man of many surprises"? Could she have said, he wanted to know, that he was "a man of many *wonderful* surprises"?

"No," I said, "I think she just said 'a man of—'"

Suddenly, out of the corner of my eye, I saw the tent flap move!

An instant later, an arm shot through the door, snatched up the flag, which was leaning against the wall, and yanked it outside.

"The flag!" I yelled.

I leaped to my feet and dived out of the tent. Through the rain I could see Jill, Sunny, and Katherine, all wearing rain jackets, heading for the big rock, on the run. Jill had the flag. It flapped in the wind as she ran.

I took off after them, with Cornelius and Pete right behind me. Squeezing around the rock slowed Katherine and the girls down, but of course it slowed us down, too. By the time we all got around to the other side, they had a good solid lead. They were crashing through the underbrush, twenty yards ahead, paralleling the shoreline.

Cornelius grabbed my shoulder. "This way!" he said, turning inland. "It's shorter."

Pete and I followed after him. It was raining harder now, and already my hair was plastered down across my forehead. I had to keep brushing it out of my eyes as we ran, scrambling and slipping over rocks and fallen trees.

When we reached the main trail, leading from Mount Mysterious to the tree house, the going got easier, even though now the storm really let loose. What a downpour! Cornelius was right in front of me, but the rain was so heavy I could hardly see him. I was soaking wet, but I didn't care. I knew we were making good time. Our feet made *splat! splat! splat!* sounds as we raced through the mud.

Suddenly, we burst out at the inlet, running so fast we almost went tumbling into the water. We looked over through the driving rain. There was the tree house. And hanging down from the middle tree was a rope ladder! We went for it.

I got there first and scrambled up the ladder, slipping once, then scrambling on, clambering up onto the platform. Cornelius was right behind me, climbing fast. I helped him up. Then Pete. He was halfway up when I saw Sunny.

She broke through the bushes over behind the first tree and sprinted toward the ladder. Wow! Could she *run*!

Cornelius and I reached down, grabbed Pete's arms, and practically jerked him up onto the platform. Sunny was closing in. As fast as I could, I began pulling the ladder up, hand over hand. Sunny leaped.

She missed the ladder by inches.

"Nice try!" said Pete, with real admiration in

his voice. And no wonder—she jumped like a professional basketball player.

And now, here came Katherine and Jill, charging out of the forest, Jill still carrying the flag. Seconds later, they arrived under our platform, huffing and puffing.

All three of them scowled up at us from under their rain hoods.

We smiled and waved.

"Hi, there!" said Cornelius with lots of charm. "So nice to see you again."

"Lower that ladder this instant!" demanded Katherine.

Cornelius whispered in my ear and I ran up to the breakfast balcony and returned with the basket and rope.

"We'd be happy to lower the ladder," said Cornelius as he peered over the edge of the platform, "just as soon as you give us the flag and we deliver it to the finish line."

"Making us the All-Time Champions, of course," Pete pointed out.

I started lowering the basket. "Just put the flag in here," I said helpfully.

Katherine swept the hood back off her head. "Over my dead body!" she burst out.

"No way!" said Jill.

143

"Not in a million years!" said Sunny.

They glared at us in silence. It was a standoff—just like before, only this time *they* had the flag, and *we* had the tree house.

Katherine turned to Jill and Sunny to say something, but suddenly she stopped and just sort of stared at them.

A change came over her face. It softened, and there was a little twitch around the corner of her mouth. I almost thought she was going to break into a grin or something.

And I could understand why she might. Jill and Sunny looked pretty funny—standing there in mud practically up to their ankles, looking so serious, with the hoods of their rain jackets tied snugly under their chins so that only the little round circles of their faces were showing. Jill was defiantly holding up the stick with the wet, limp, Snowball-and-Poopsie flag on it.

Katherine let out a chuckle. She tried to stifle it, but it was a chuckle, all right.

Jill and Sunny heard it.

"*What's so funny?*" Jill demanded. She waved the flag around and it went flapping into Sunny's face, making a wet, slapping sound.

That did it. Katherine cracked up.

"If you two could see yourselves!" she managed to say, giggling.

Jill and Sunny looked at each other in aston-
ishment. I thought they were going to get mad
or something. But after a few seconds, they started
giggling, too.

Jill looked up at us. *"And look at them!"* she
whooped, pointing.

Katherine and Sunny and Jill broke into gales
of laughter.

I couldn't help laughing myself. I guess we did
look pretty goofy, standing up there trying to
look like All-Time Champions, dripping wet, with
our blue jeans all splattered with mud and our
hair plastered down flat on our heads.

Before I knew it, Pete and Cornelius joined in,
too. In fact, they laughed so hard they had to sit
down to keep from falling off the platform.

Then Jill held out the flag so we could all see
it. *"Look!"* she sort of gasped in between giggles.

I guess the marker pens Pete had used when
he made the flag weren't waterproof, because the
rain had sure taken its toll. Snowball and Poopsie
had become one big, runny, turtlelike blob.

That set us all off again.

And as we were laughing, I found myself
thinking about Jill and Sunny and Katherine—
and I found myself really liking them. All of them.
One thing was for sure: they really knew how to
have fun. And they were good sports, too.

Now Katherine was goofing off, doing a little dance in the mud. Boy, did she look funny tap-dancing in her hiking boots. Pete fell over backward on the platform, hiccuping.

All of a sudden, an idea came to me.

I leaned over and whispered to Cornelius. At first he looked surprised, but then he nodded. "A fine idea," he said. He turned and whispered to Pete—and I saw Pete nod in agreement, still hiccuping.

Cornelius stood up.

"Ladies," he said dramatically, "I have a proposal to make."

Katherine stopped dancing, and the three of them looked up at him.

"Actually," Cornelius went on, "it's Scott's proposal, but Pete and I have given it our full approval. The three of us—the Turtle Island Trailblazers, as we like to call ourselves—suggest that we declare this race a tie. No winners, no losers, no hard feelings. What do you say?"

There was a short pause.

"And no tricks?" asked Jill.

"No tricks," said Cornelius.

Katherine and the girls put their heads together and talked it over. Finally, they looked back up at us.

"You've got a deal," said Jill.

"Why not?" said Sunny.

"Sounds good to me," said Katherine. "I'd do anything for a cup of hot chocolate along about now."

We grinned, and Pete and I began lowering the rope ladder.

The Great Turtle Island Flag Race was over.

23

A shooting star streaked across the northern sky.

"Ah, peace and harmony!" exclaimed Cornelius. "Isn't it wonderful, boys, to have peace and harmony once again on Turtle Island?"

It was just after midnight, and Cornelius, Pete, and I were up on the moon-viewing platform. This was the peak night for the Perseid meteor shower, and it was really putting on a show.

Katherine and the girls had left a few hours earlier, after we'd all had some hot chocolate up in the tree house. Of course, Cornelius, Pete, and I had changed into some dry clothes first. Pete and I didn't have any extra clothes with us, so we had to borrow some things from Cornelius that were quite a bit too large, to put it mildly. They made us look sort of like balloons, and we kept tripping over our pants cuffs.

"Wow!" said Jill when she saw us. She gave a low whistle. "You two look *adorable*."

She suggested we drop by their camp the next day, dressed the same way, so she could take our pictures.

"Sorry," I said, "but we only wear these outfits on special occasions. Like tonight. And Halloween."

Later, before Katherine and the girls headed back to their camp, we all agreed to meet at nine o'clock the next morning on top of Mount Mysterious. Cornelius was going to show us a cave. It was on the side of the hill, he said, with an entrance so nearly hidden that it had taken him three summers to discover it. Inside the cave, he told us, were two chambers, and on the walls of the inner one were some very strange and puzzling Indian pictographs. He said he knew we were going to like it.

Pete right away named it Dead Indian Cave. Sunny said she thought Wild Horse Hideaway was a better name. Pete said he didn't think so. Sunny said she *did* think so. After a lot of discussion, they settled on Dead Indian's Wild Horse Hideaway.

When Katherine and the girls finally left, we stood on the balcony, watching as the light from their flashlights disappeared into the night. Cornelius leaned on the railing and sighed.

"What a woman!" I heard him murmur.

It had been a long and eventful day. And now, up on the moon-viewing platform, Cornelius was beginning to get philosophical.

"Boys," he said grandly, "you have done something today you can be proud of. Think about it! In spite of all your previous problems with Jill and Sunny, you have built a strong, enduring friendship with them. You have done this even though they took your pictures in certain . . . well . . . embarrassing situations—like falling out of your canoe, and belly-flopping in the mud, and getting stuck in the window of your Gingerbread Tent. Yes, in spite of all this, you were still able to meet them halfway. You have let bygones be bygones. You have, in short, made two good friends and restored peace and harmony to Turtle Island."

He paused dramatically, and then added, "I'm proud of you."

I didn't know what to say.

"Uh, thanks," I said.

"It was nothing," said Pete.

"And won't it be fun," said Cornelius, "when we all meet on top of Mount Mysterious tomorrow morning and explore Dead Indian's Wild Horse Hideaway together?"

"It does sound like fun," I admitted.

"Are there any bats?" asked Pete.

"Plenty of them," said Cornelius.

We watched the shooting stars in silence for a while, and as we did, I got to thinking about the next day—and chuckled to myself. You see, actually, Pete and I were going to be a few minutes late to the meeting on Mount Mysterious. We'd already made plans to take care of a little business first. Bright and early the next morning, we were going to be hiding in the tall grass on the ridge above the girls' camp. As soon as they left for Mount Mysterious, we were going to make a short, quick commando raid on their tent—*to get those pictures!*

And, while we were there, we thought maybe we'd take the time to stuff their sleeping bags full of leaves and lily pads.

After all, we wouldn't want *too* much peace and harmony on Turtle Island, would we?